PENGUIN CLASSICS

THE LIFE AND ADVENTURES OF JOAQUÍN MURIETA

JOHN ROLLIN RIDGE (1827–1867), also known as Yellow Bird, was born in Georgia to a Cherokee father, who was murdered by a Cherokee leader for having supported the treaty that led to the Trail of Tears. After killing a man who had stolen his horse, Ridge fled to California, where he identified with Mexican Americans who had been displaced from their land by white settlers. He wrote for the *San Francisco Herald*, among other publications, and was the first editor of the *Sacramento Bee*. His only novel, *The Life and Adventures of Joaquín Murieta*, was published in 1854.

HSUAN L. HSU is a professor of English at the University of California, Davis. He is the author of *Sitting in Darkness: Mark Twain's Asia and Comparative Racialization* and *Geography and the Production of Space in Nineteenth-Century American Literature* and the editor of the Broadview Press editions of *Pudd'nhead Wilson and Those Extraordinary Twins* by Mark Twain and *Mrs. Spring Fragrance* by Sui Sin Far (Edith Maude Eaton).

DIANA GABALDON is the author of the multimillion-copy #1 *New York Times* bestselling Outlander series. She lives in Scottsdale, Arizona, with her husband.

JOHN ROLLIN RIDGE

The Life and Adventures of Joaquín Murieta

THE CELEBRATED CALIFORNIA BANDIT

Edited with an Introduction and Notes by
HSUAN L. HSU

Foreword by
DIANA GABALDON

PENGUIN BOOKS

PENGUIN BOOKS

An imprint of Penguin Random House LLC
375 Hudson Street
New York, New York 10014
penguinrandomhouse.com

First published in the United States of America by W. B. Cooke, San Francisco, 1854
This edition with an introduction and notes by Hsuan L. Hsu and a foreword by
Diana Gabaldon published in Penguin Books 2018

Image on p. 138: W. C. Butler, "Death of Joaquín," illustration reproduced from Unsigned,
The Life of Joaquín Murieta, the Brigand Chief of California (California Police Gazette), p. 67.
Courtesy of The Bancroft Library, University of California, Berkeley.

LIBRARY OF CONGRESS CATALOGING-IN-PUBLICATION DATA
Names: Ridge, John Rollin, 1827–1867, author. | Hsu, Hsuan L., 1976– editor.
| Gabaldon, Diana, writer of foreword.
Title: The life and adventures of Joaquin Murieta : the celebrated California
bandit / John Rollin Ridge ; edited with an introduction and notes by
Hsuan L. Hsu ; foreword by Diana Gabaldon.
Description: New York : Penguin Books, [2018] | Includes bibliographical
references.
Identifiers: LCCN 2018013787 (print) | LCCN 2018016507 (ebook) |
ISBN 9780525504580 (ebook) | ISBN 9780143132653 (print)
Subjects: LCSH: Murieta, Joaquâin, -1853—Fiction. | Frontier and pioneer
life—Fiction. | Revolutionaries—Fiction. | Outlaws—Fiction. |
California—Fiction. | Biographical fiction. | Western stories.
Classification: LCC PS2699.R75 (ebook) | LCC PS2699.R75 L54 2018 (print) |
DDC 813/.4—dc23
LC record available at https://lccn.loc.gov/2018013787

Printed in the United States of America

ScoutAutomatedPrintCode

Set in Sabon LT Std

Contents

Foreword

My father loved Zorro. He also identified strongly with another Hispanic outlaw-hero, Speedy Gonzales, the Warner Bros. cartoon mouse with ADHD who ran rings around authority. Reading this book, I kept wondering what he would have thought of Joaquín Murieta.

My dad was the youngest of thirteen children born to a New Mexican dirt farmer (hence the expression "dirt poor"). His first language was Spanish, and—having been born in 1930—he experienced a fair amount of discrimination, like most "Mexicans"* at the time. When

---

* "Mexican" is an odd designation. Sometimes it has the traditional meaning: a person who either lives/lived in Mexico or is directly descended from the people(s)—note that plural—of Mexico. Most often in present times in the US, it's a catch-all term for any person of Hispanic descent (even though a great many such people come—especially in recent years—from places like El Salvador, Guatemala, Ecuador, and Chile; also Cuba, but Cubans are geographically localized and have a strong community with a distinct identity).

For what it's worth, my nine-times great-grandfather traveled from Toledo, Spain, to Mexico City in 1679. His two sons traveled north to Santa Fe and settled there in 1705, and the family pretty much stayed in that area for the next 250 years. So . . . in 1679, Mexico (the entire territory, which included most of present-day New Mexico was (politically) New Spain, and its inhabitants (whatever their genetic makeup) were citizens of Spain.

They stayed Spaniards until the end of the War of Mexican Independence, in 1821. At this point, my paternal ancestors became Mexicans—for the next thirty years, at which point the Treaty of Guadalupe-Hidalgo (1848) ceded the New Mexico Territory to the US, and we became

my parents became engaged, in 1948, in Flagstaff, Arizona, public petitions against their marriage were circulated (my mother was not only Anglo, she was also the mayor's daughter—you can see why my dad liked Zorro, who always put one over on the *alcalde*), and at one point, my mother's high-school English teacher took her aside and said, "You can't marry that man—your children will be idiots!"

In recent years, it has struck me as funny (both in an ironic way and just that it's really funny) that both Zorro and Speedy are now perceived (by the sorts of people who spend their time thinking about such things) as racist stereotypes, because I've never personally met a "Mexican" who thought that. When does a positive identification with iconic virtue become a racist stereotype? I suppose it depends on the viewpoint of the person concerned.

Personally, as a child I liked the Zorro sword, but the hat with the dangly bobbles wasn't me. Just as well: Given the crack about idiots, my dad wouldn't have let me run around dressed like Zorro. I had a gender-appropriate Annie Oakley costume, complete with fringed skirt and pearl (plastic)-handled six-guns with holsters. The whole family liked Speedy Gonzales, though—especially Dad, an award-winning high-school athlete who became a state senator.

My dad liked outlaws, but he played it straight; he worked hard and was good at what he did. One reason for the popularity of outlaw-heroes is that they're competent. Joaquín has that one down. Nobody outshoots, outrides, or out-flamboyants him, and the only man ever to get the drop on him (until The End) is an Indian chief.

_____

Americans, all without moving a step. (My maternal ancestors—mostly English, with one odd German branch—didn't arrive in America until the 1700s, the laggards. . . .)

But there's got to be a bit more to it than the simple joy of seeing a job well done, even if said job is robbing and killing Chinese miners. I did a quick search for "Mexican folk heroes," as, frankly, off the top of my head, I couldn't think of any—unless you count Pancho Villa (in my youth, I could sing—in Spanish—all the verses of "La Cucaracha," but that would be the sum total of my cultural associations with *Señor* Villa). I suppose we could include Don Quixote, for the sake of argument, but, really, there aren't any Hispanic folk heroes to speak of until we get to the twentieth century and Cesar Chavez (whom I met at the age of sixteen or so—I was sixteen, I mean; he was in his fifties)—and he was an American, not a Mexican, and not generally an outlaw.

So we're kind of back to the fictional Mexican/Latino/Hispanic/whatever heroes. Most of whom seem to be outlaws. This is reasonable: A good folk hero defends common people against the oppression of the local (usually corrupt) power structure, and it's generally the power structure that's making the laws.

Likewise, nothing creates a sense of fellowship more than a joint sense of oppression by a common enemy. This is why outlaws often have a gang (or at least a sidekick to whom they confide their plans). And in most cases, these gangs share an identity, whether it's based on race, social class, or merely having the sort of personality that keeps you from holding down a job.

Zorro and Speedy were pretty much loners, though they did have valets, sidekicks, or friends to help out with the incidental logistics of their plans. Don Quixote, of course, had Sancho Panza. Joaquín's plans are a bit more grandiose, though, and he has a large gang, though he mostly operates with just a few close confederates—all of them Mexicans.

Now, we have certain requirements of heroes. They

can't be selfish; they must always be concerned for others. This means that outlaw-heroes walk a fine line; yes, we approve of (or at least sympathize with) them robbing, harassing, or even killing people we consider "oppressors" (whether of ourselves or others), but we don't make heroes of outlaws whose chief motive seems to be their own enrichment. (Outlaws who are in it for the buck are fascinating and/or romantic—*vide* Bonnie and Clyde, John Dillinger, etc.—but not usually heroic.)

In *The Life and Adventures of Joaquín Murieta,* John Rollin Ridge finessed this one by introducing (rather belatedly, if you ask me) the notion that Joaquín was not stealing everything not nailed down for his own enrichment, but was in fact planning a great military action that would "sweep the Americans from his [Joaquín's] land"—i.e., California. To this end, he was collecting horses—obviously a logical first move. Mind you, he never does anything else toward his ultimate goal, like collecting guns, organizing a militia, or recruiting men to feed—let alone ride—the thousands of horses he's stashing away in his arroyo hideout, but occasional brief references to his grand scheme are theoretically sufficient to excuse the theme and variation of ambush, robbery, murder, and daring escape.

To me, one of the most interesting aspects of the book is its charmingly casual racism. Racism is Joaquín's chief *modus operandi.* White people are Bad, Mexicans are Good. Chinamen [*sic*] are very industrious but stink at fighting, so naturally you should rob them whenever you come across them because they always have gold and it's easy. Sometimes you kill them, too, but that's not much fun.

Non-Chinese miners are usually tough, wary, and well armed—but lots more fun to rob and kill. Indians? They're

as tough as Mexicans, less well armed, but better organized. Worthy and honorable foes, but they don't have any
money. And, of course, they don't have any money because
they're oppressed by the white intruders, thus forming a
bond of fellowship with Joaquín and company. (It's worth
noting at this point that Ridge was himself half-Cherokee
and considered himself an Indian, which may have had
something to do with this distinction.)

Frankly, I've seen this kind of matter-of-fact racism all
my life; most people my age probably have. There's usually no particular animus to it; it's just people calling it
like they see it—and how (and why) they see it is really
interesting.

Ridge's book was published in 1854, slightly pre–Civil
War. How old is the idea of the equality of all men before
God? It's not that old. Socrates, Aristotle, all the virtuous
old Greeks and Romans kept slaves as a matter of course,
and the writers of the US Constitution—their noble language notwithstanding—considered slaves to be not only
legal but also a fraction of a free man, for census and
taxation purposes.

I've always thought that the interest (and value) of a
historical piece of fiction lies in its reflection of the pre-
vailing cultural values. How did people think in this period? Why did they believe what they did, and how did
those beliefs shape their lives?

Historical fiction, however, is different from fiction
from an earlier era. We don't like to think our heroes
didn't believe the same things we believe, so contempo-
rary fiction written about an earlier time often reflects
the perceived attitude of the intended audience rather than
the actual cultural context of the period.

Frankly, the political ideology of the twenty-first century goes hand-in-hand with a deliberate ignorance of the

past, and depends upon it. It's interesting to note that for authors writing historical fiction today, there's considerable pressure to avoid showing cultural attitudes as they actually existed—or, if shown, to attribute these attitudes only to characters clearly drawn as despicable.

Ridge didn't suffer from such considerations: He had nothing even faintly idealistic in mind, nor was he concerned with improving social values. It's debatable— given his chronic poverty and lack of success in other endeavors—whether we might reasonably conclude that he wrote *Joaquín Murieta* for the primary purpose of making money, or whether we should accept his claim that the book is intended as a modest contribution to the history of California. In either case, the attitudes he depicts were almost certainly the attitudes he perceived his potential audience as having. Of course he wasn't writing historical fiction, but in writing about his own time he offers a really good view of the cultural context he lived in and his own audience—which is now, of course, historical.

The book is remarkably readable and entertaining, despite the Victorian style. Ridge is a master of the art of theme and variation, so while every encounter ends the same way (until The End), we still enjoy the ride. If you want to read a little deeper, though, the story offers a window on the real social dynamics—race, culture, and prejudices—of the time, and may offer grounds for reflection on how much things have changed. Or haven't.

In the end, I don't think Dad would have approved of Joaquín. Not because Joaquín had attitudes characteristic of his times—my dad was a politician; he understood how people worked—but because he wasn't responsible. True, he'd go rescue a friend who was about to be hanged, but he doesn't take care of his woman, and in the end he leaves her penniless and bereft, living in her parents' home. (Cf. attitudes of the times. Women weren't interesting, beyond an occasional static role as a plot point.) And worst of all . . . he lets his pride get the better of him, and ends up with his head in a bottle.

In my dad's view of things, the good ones don't end up in a bottle. That sad end was apparently not only Joaquín's but also the author's. Ridge died at an early age of "softening of the brain" (i.e., probably acute alcoholism), but his novel lives on, both as rip-roaring entertainment and as social commentary that Ridge probably didn't intend. But books are immortal, and have minds of their own.

DIANA GABALDON

Introduction

Like its elusive hero, *The Life and Adventures of Joaquín Murieta, the Celebrated California Bandit* (1854) is difficult to pin down. It has the distinction of being the first novel published in California, the first novel published by a Native American, and the first American novel to feature a Mexican protagonist. Its story draws together transformational events in the history of three nations, connecting the California Gold Rush with the Cherokee Trail of Tears and the US-Mexican War. It blends elements of epic, folk tale, revenge tragedy, and romance—yet historians have often treated it as a factual record. It has been repurposed, and sometimes plagiarized, throughout the US, Mexico, Europe, and Latin America; in publications ranging from the *California Police Gazette* to the popular *Corrido de Joaquín Murrieta*, a play by the Chilean poet Pablo Neruda; and the 1998 Hollywood film *The Mask of Zorro* (in which Joaquín's brother, played by Antonio Banderas, takes up the mask of Zorro). While few Americans today would recognize the name of Joaquín Murieta, most are familiar with figures such as Zorro and Batman, whose creators were inspired by this sensational account of vigilante justice and righteous violence. Paradoxically, John Rollin Ridge's book (published under his Cherokee name, Yellow Bird) has become both one of the most influential and one of the most invisible novels in the history of American literature.

In addition to its profound and wide-ranging cultural influence, *Joaquín Murieta* is distinguished by Ridge's formal and thematic ambitions. Formally, Ridge stretches the conventions of sensational crime fiction to plot not just the rapid and mysterious movements of his protagonist across California's sparsely settled landscapes, but also Murieta's conflicted character and the ideological tensions between individual and collective motives. The novel's formal idiosyncrasies—interpolating a landscape poem; jumping around in space and time; and shifting among the perspectives of Murieta, the minor characters who comprise his organization, and the men who try to hunt him down—express the social frictions at the heart of Ridge's concerns. Meanwhile, *Joaquín Murieta* takes up some of the most complex themes in American literature: cultural assimilation, racist and antiracist violence, the tension between ethical and political action, and—perhaps most centrally—philosophical questions about the legitimacy of state and extralegal violence. It stands alongside such works as Nat Turner and Thomas Gray's *The Confessions of Nat Turner* (1831), William Apess's "Eulogy on King Philip" (1836), Herman Melville's "Benito Cereno" (1855), Frederick Douglass's *The Heroic Slave,* Harriet Beecher Stowe's *Dred: A Tale of the Great Dismal Swamp,* and Martin R. Delany's *Blake; or, The Huts of America* (1859) as a classic American story of antiracist insurrection.

The "Publishers' Preface" to the 1854 edition inaugurated one influential model for reading *Joaquín Murieta* by suggesting that the novel reflects "the tragical events" and "civil commotion" precipitated by the federal government's removal of the Cherokee Nation from their ancestral lands. In the wake of the estimated four thousand

Cherokee deaths resulting from the Trail of Tears, nego-
tiations with the US government caused intense ideological conflict among the Cherokee. Ridge's father (John
Ridge), grandfather (Major Ridge), and cousin (Elias
Boudinot) were prominent Cherokee leaders who believed that the only way to protect the Cherokee Nation's
rights was to negotiate a treaty with the federal government. Without the approval of the Cherokee National
Council or Principal Chief John Ross, they signed the
1835 Treaty of New Echota, which ceded the Cherokee
Nation's territory in the southeast and established a basis
for forced removal. In 1839, when Ridge was twelve years
old, a group of Ross's supporters assassinated Ridge's father, his grandfather, and Boudinot for having signed the
treaty; in the lurid terms of the Publishers' Preface,
"While the bleeding corpse of his father was yet lying in
the house, surrounded by his weeping family, the news
came that his grand-father, a distinguished old war-chief,
was also killed; and, fast upon this report, that others of
his near relatives were slain." Ridge's mother (Sarah Bird
Northrup, a white woman) fled with her children to Fay-
etteville, Arkansas, where Ridge studied law. In 1849
Ridge killed a Ross sympathizer named David Kell in a
horse dispute, and fled the state. He moved to California
to join the Gold Rush in 1850, but soon gave up mining
to work as a poet, journalist, and the editor of several
newspapers.*

In California, Ridge witnessed a young state shot
through with social contradictions and upheavals. California had been transferred to the US under the terms of
the Treaty of Guadalupe-Hidalgo, which concluded the
US-Mexico War (1846–48). The treaty stipulated that

---

* Parins, *John Rollin Ridge: His Life and Works*, pp. 1–94, provides a
detailed account of Ridge's early years.

Mexican inhabitants of the territory could choose to remain in California and receive US citizenship, and the
majority of California's Mexican inhabitants chose to remain. However, California's constitution restricted voting rights to white men (thus disenfranchising Mexicans
of black or Native descent), and the federal government
failed to honor the property rights of former Mexican
citizens. In the same years, the California Gold Rush led
to rapid growth, as miners from all over the world swelled
the non-Native population from 15,000 in 1848 to
165,000 in 1850.* By contrast, this influx of settlers
brought about a catastrophic decline in the state's Native
population. "From 1846 to 1873, colonization policies,
abductions, diseases, homicides, executions, battles, massacres, institutionalized neglect on federal reservations,
and the willful destruction of indigenous villages and
their food stores seem to have reduced California Indian
numbers by at least 80 percent, from perhaps 150,000 to
some 30,000."† The nascent state government quickly
moved to legislate white supremacy by imposing racially
targeted laws. In 1849 General Persifor Smith, the US
military governor of California, sanctioned the rumor
that it was illegal for non-citizens to dig gold in the state.
In addition, voting rights were withheld, black and (later)
Chinese witnesses were prohibited from testifying in
court, Native Americans charged with "vagrancy" were
subjected to forced labor, and in 1850 California instituted a Foreign Miners' Tax that was chiefly (and often
violently) enforced against Mexican, South American,
and eventually Chinese miners. (In the novel, Ridge refers to the last of these outrages when he describes

* McWilliams, *California: The Great Exception*, p. 66.

† Madley, *An American Genocide: The United States and the California
Indian Catastrophe, 1846–1873*, p. 346.

Murieta's robbery of a group of Germans as "collect[ing] taxes off of them for 'Foreign Miners' Licenses.'") Racially motivated lynchings and other forms of mob violence such as those depicted in Ridge's novel were common occurrences. In 1851 Native Cahuilla and Cupeño warriors conducted a series of raids in Southern California before their alleged leader, Antonio Garra, was captured and executed. Newspaper accounts of the "Garra Uprising," which reported that the charismatic leader was secretly aided by *Californios,* may have informed Ridge's account of Murieta's activities.*

Although Ridge advocated for the rights of the Cherokee Nation and Mexican Americans in his writings, his ideas about race and identity were complex and often incoherent. Ridge did not believe in the equality of races. Descended from a family of slaveholders (Ridge had held slaves while living in Arkansas), he opposed both abolitionism and the Civil War. In *Joaquín Murieta* he depicts California Indians as uncivilized cowards and presents titillating descriptions of well-known bandit Three-Fingered Jack's brutal massacres of passive Chinese miners.† Even among his characters of Mexican descent, Ridge distinguishes between the nobility of Murieta (whose "complexion was neither very dark nor very light") and the frequently ignoble, undisciplined character of his followers. In his newspaper writings, he endorsed amalgamation and cultural assimilation as the best path forward for Native Americans. Whereas many Native Americans emphasized the importance of sovereignty and

* Rifkin, "'For the Wrongs of Our Poor Bleeding Country': Sensation, Class, and Empire in Ridge's *Joaquín Murieta,*" p. 38.

† On Ridge's depiction of cross-racial interactions, see Christensen, "Minority Interaction in John Rollin Ridge's *The Life and Adventures of Joaquín Murieta.*"

self-determination, Ridge believed that more "civilized" Native groups such as the Cherokee were worthy of the rights and privileges of US citizenship.* He also "shared with many Euro-Americans the racist assumption that intermarriage between whites and Natives was a necessary precondition for 'civilizing' indigenous peoples."† This may explain why, by contrast with the Tejon Indians, the "half-breeds" at Cherokee Flat provide such effective support (in the form of torture and extrajudicial executions) to Captain Ellas in his search for Murieta's men.

The Life and Adventures of Joaquín Murieta is Ridge's novelization of a series of sensational newspaper accounts of Mexican bandits robbing white and Asian miners and travelers between 1851 and 1853. The name "Joaquín Murieta"‡ refers to just one of many men accused of leading these bandit organizations. There were at least five Joaquíns who figured prominently in accounts of Mexican bandit raids. In 1853 the California legislature authorized Captain Harry Love to organize a group of twenty Rangers and lead them to capture "the party or gang of robbers commanded by the five Joaquins, whose names are Joaquin Muriati, Ocomorenia, Valenzuela, Botellier, and Carillo, and their band of associates."§ When Love and his Rangers killed several Mexican horse thieves in a gunfight on July 25 of that year, they decapitated one of the corpses and preserved the head in alcohol along with a hand supposedly belonging to Three-Fingered Jack. The head was

---

* Whitley, "The First White Aboriginal," p. 126.

† Whitley, p. 111.

‡ Also spelled "Murrieta." This introduction will use "Murieta," the spelling that Ridge used.

§ Hausman, "Becoming Joaquin Murrieta: John Rollin Ridge and the Making of an Icon," p. 32.

displayed across the state as that of "Joaquin Murrieta."
While Love and his Rangers claimed $6,000 in reward
money for securing this trophy, some commentators questioned its authenticity. For example, a review of Ridge's
novel in San Francisco's *Daily California Chronicle* suggested that "The book may serve as very amusing reading
for Joaquín Murieta, should he get hold of it, for notwithstanding all which has been said and published to the contrary, we have little faith in his reported death at the hands
of Love's party."* But for those who did believe Love's
claims, the preserved head retroactively singled out Murieta as the most notorious of the five Joaquíns and the
most celebrated of California's Mexican bandits.

For both aesthetic and political reasons, Ridge's novel af-
firms that the preserved head was Murieta's, and insists
upon his hero's individual responsibility for crimes that occurred throughout the state. Condensing the activities of
scattered bandit groups into a single organization led by a
man of extraordinary capacities, Ridge gave social disorder
a perceptible shape and a storyline with a beginning and
an end. Representing Murieta and Three-Fingered Jack as
extraordinary, mythical figures, he fit them into familiar
conventions such as the romantic youth, the chivalric ad-
venturer, and the sadistic murderer. This double representation of Mexican bandits as a combination of noble hero
(Murieta) and murderous monster (Three-Fingered Jack)
elicits readers' sympathy for Murieta while also suggesting
the need for vigilante methods for suppressing the bandits.
What begins as a story about a heroic insurrectionary
against white supremacy becomes an ambivalent argument
for the judicious deployment of extralegal violence—a

* Parins, p. 104. Ridge published a rebuttal in which he claimed the
novel was based on newspaper files and conversations with witnesses
throughout the state (Parins, p. 105).

justification of, as Ridge writes in the novel, "discretionary power, so necessary to be used in perilous times when the slow forms of law . . . are altogether useless and inefficient."

Packed with melodrama, bravado, daring escapes, and graphic violence, Ridge's short novel (the first edition, published by San Francisco's W. B. Cooke, was just ninety pages) traces Murieta's transformation from a young Mexican immigrant into a legendary bandit and insurrectionary. Murieta starts off as an "exceedingly handsome and attractive" young man who arrives in California "fired with enthusiastic admiration of the American character." Like the young Ridge, he is displaced, assaulted, and forced to witness assaults on his family when white men jump his claim, rape his wife, take his farm, murder his half-brother, and publicly whip him. After numerous attempts to live an honest life in the face of racial violence, Murieta turns outlaw, kills all the men in the mob that assaulted him, and organizes a statewide network of bandits secretly aided by Mexican civilians. A master of disguise, a brilliant tactician, and an eloquent speaker, he unfolds a plan to raise and supply a band of "fifteen hundred or two thousand men" for a mass raid of southern California: "to kill the Americans by 'wholesale,' burn their ranchos, and run off their property at one single swoop so rapidly that they will not have time to collect an opposing force before I will have finished the work and found safety in the mountains of Sonora." His own suffering at the hands of white attackers represents the plight of all Mexicans whose rights went unprotected following the Treaty of Guadalupe-Hidalgo: "My brothers, we will then be revenged for our wrongs, and some little, too, for the wrongs of our poor, bleeding country." After narrating a series of adventures, run-ins with the military, near misses, massacres of "Chinamen," and incidents illustrating Murieta's noble character, Ridge shifts to an account of numerous efforts to hunt down the bandits. The outcome of Harry Love's campaign, in which Murieta's head and Three-Fingered Jack's hand are preserved and exhibited around the state, would not have been news to many of the novel's nineteenth-century readers. What would have come as more of a surprise is Ridge's interpretation of the story: "there is nothing so dangerous in its consequences as *injustice to individuals*—whether it arise from prejudice of color or from any other source . . . a wrong done to one man is a wrong to society and to the world."

Like the Westerns and vigilante narratives it influenced, *Joaquín Murieta* presents a conflicted drama about the legitimacy of violence in a time and place where the rule of law was not firmly established. In the novel, conflicts are settled by mob rule, extrajudicial "trains," inequitable laws, vigilante policing, and summary lynchings rather than by the courts. Under such chaotic conditions, justice depends on the discretion of righteous individuals. For example, Murieta takes justice into his own hands when he kills the men who flogged him, when he plots revenge for the wrongs committed against all Mexicans, when he decides not to steal from a poor ferryman, when a well-spoken youth persuades him to spare a group of hunters, and when he returns a kidnapped woman to her mother and fiancé. At times, Ridge presents his hero's ethical deliberations, retributive killings, forcible collection of "tributes" from white and Chinese miners, and cautious governance of his outlaw followers as a kind of shadow government that enacts Murieta's vision of justice in the absence of just laws. Murieta's virtue, however, has clear limits. This is most evident when he allows Three-Fingered Jack to torture and kill Chinese

men indiscriminately because he cannot attain his aims
without Three-Fingered Jack's support. Murieta's belief
that the ends justify the means is difficult to distinguish
from the vigilante tactics of his pursuers, who torture
and execute Mexicans suspected of aiding the bandits
without due process.

In the novel, Murieta is mirrored by his most formidable pursuers, Captains Charles Ellas and Harry Love.
Ellas emerges as a counterweight to the intensification of
the bandits' activities in 1853: "so diverse were their operations, so numerous and swift, that I shall not attempt
to give a minute account of them," writes Ridge. Ellas, a
courageous, active, and honorable "young man of fine
appearance," is "naturally looked to as a leader" by the
terrified populace. Like Murieta, however, Ellas finds
himself torn between his "chivalrous" character and the
exigencies of his mission. He relies on information acquired through the arbitrary detention, torture, and murder of suspicious-looking Mexicans, and (like Murieta)
he delegates these methods to others: "A doubt arising in
the minds of some persons . . . as to whether it was right
to put the fellow to death, Ellas left him in charge of the
two Cherokee half-breeds with the request that they
would give a good account of him. . . ." The two litho-
graphs included in the first edition (see pages 6 and 75),
portraits of Murieta and Love, invite readers to compare
the bandit with the man who killed him. Ridge describes
Love as Murieta's counterpart, an energetic and "stealthy
pursuer" whose "brain was as strong and clear in the
midst of dangers as that of the daring robber against
whom he was sent, and who possessed a glance as quick
and a hand as sudden in the execution of a deadly purpose." If the state's agents of discretionary violence ap-
pear to help establish the rule of law, they also spread
chaos and insecurity. With armed parties scouring the

countryside, "Arrests were continually being made; popular tribunals established in the woods, Judge Lynch installed upon the bench; criminals arraigned, tried, and
executed upon the limb of a tree; pursuits, flights, skirmishes, and a topsy-turvy, hurly-burly mass of events
that set narration of defiance." Even the suspected "harboring places and dens of the robbers"—presumably the
homes of Mexican non-combatants—are systematically
destroyed and burned by a mob of angry citizens. While
Ridge generally uses the distancing techniques of euphe-
mism and passive voice to describe atrocities committed
in the name of the law, at one point he breaks off his narrative to offer an ironic commentary on the "custom" of
lynching: "Bah! it is a sight that I never like to see, although I have been civilized for a good many years."

In the last sixty-plus years since the novel's 1955 republica-
tion, critics have come to interpret Ridge's novel variously
as a folk story of a charismatic Robin Hood–like bandit,
an impassioned protest against racial injustice, a troubled
justification of state violence, a thinly veiled plotting of
Ridge's personal revenge fantasies, an allegory of the tensions between ethnic assimilation and anticolonial resistance, and a foundational work of Native American and
California literature.* These readings explore important
questions about the novel's significance: Does Murieta
stand in for the wounded and vengeful Mexican body politic, or does he unravel Mexican group identity by embracing an individualist and elitist individualism?† Does his
ability to move undetected throughout California em-
power him, or does it give license to the state's deployment

---

* See, e.g., Jackson, Rifkin, Owens, Rowe, Smith, and Walker.

† See Aleman, "Assimilation and the Decapitated Body Politic in *The Life
and Adventures of Joaquín Murieta.*"

of extraordinary police powers? If Three-Fingered Jack's violence and lack of self-restraint represent the antithesis of Murieta's noble character, what are we to make of the fact that Murieta's plans depend on Three-Fingered Jack's brutality?* If *Joaquín Murieta* allegorizes the injustices experienced by the Cherokee, why does Ridge depict Cherokees torturing suspects to help hunt down the bandits?† Does the novel evoke the need for impartial law and "pure administration" (in the words of Ridge's romantic poem about Mount Shasta included in the novel), or does it advocate for natural rights and individualist ethics as opposed to legal doctrine?‡ Does Ridge represent women as objects and prizes fought over by men, or does his portrayal of the stealthy murder of an abusive bandit by the bandit's wife represent a woman heroically taking justice into her own hands?§

Critics have also traced *Joaquín Murieta*'s diverse influences across genres, media, and national boundaries.¶ Ridge's intention "to contribute my mite to those materials out of which the early history of California shall one day be composed" was eventually realized when historians—many of them influenced by Hubert Howe Bancroft's *History of California* (1882)—cited his fictional narrative as a factual record. Although the novel

---

* See Stevens, "Three-Fingered Jack and the Severed Literary History of John Rollin Ridge's *The Life and Adventures of Joaquín Murieta.*"

† Hausman, pp. 15–18.

‡ See Walker, *Indian Nation: Native American Literature and Nineteenth-Century Nationalisms,* pp. 111–38, and Rowe, "Highway Robbery: 'Indian Removal,' the Mexican-American War, and American Identity in 'The Life and Adventures of Joaquín Murieta.'"

§ See Windell, "Sanctify Our Suffering World with Tears: Transamerican Sentimentalism in *Joaquín Murieta.*"

¶ For more extensive discussions of the many reworkings of Ridge's novel, see Donahue, Hausman, Irwin, Leal, and Streeby.

was not widely reviewed upon its 1854 release, the *California Police Gazette* serialized a plagiarized version in 1859 under the title *The Life of Joaquin Murieta, the Brigand Chief of California*. This version, which demonized Murieta by omitting some of Ridge's psychological and legal explanations for Murieta's motives, was a popular success and became the source for numerous dime novels, such as *Joaquin the Saddle King: A Romance of Murieta's First Fight* (1881) and *The Pirate of the Placers; or, Joaquin's Death Hunt* (1882). (In 1871 a posthumous "Third Edition," revised and expanded by Ridge, was published by Frederick MacCrellish; in his preface, Ridge claimed that his intention was to correct the misrepresentations propagated by these derivative versions, which he referred to as "the spurious work, with its crude interpolations, fictitious additions and imperfectly disguised distortions of the author's phraseology. . . ."*) Published during the Great Depression and adapted as a film by MGM in 1936, Walter Noble Burns's *The Robin Hood of El Dorado* (1932) helped to revive Ridge's portrayal of Murieta as a hero fighting for the poor and downtrodden. This revival of interest in Murieta gave rise to both popular manifestations—such as a 1949 *Western True Crime* comic book adaptation and the George Sherman film *Murieta!* (Pro Artis Ibérica, 1965)—and the influential University of Oklahoma Press edition of *Joaquín Murieta* published in 1955. Ridge's novel has also been profoundly influential as an unambiguous representation of anticolonial resistance and resurgent cultural nationalism in Mexican American, Mexican, and South American literature and culture. The popular ballad "El Corrido de Joaquin Murrieta," for example, depicts the

---

* Ridge, *The Life and Adventures of Joaquín Murieta, the Celebrated California Bandit* (1871), p. iii.

bandit chief as a fearless enforcer of higher law who appears in saloons "punishing Anglos" while wrongly condemned by the state's "unjust laws": "Ay, que leyes tan injustas / fue llamarme bandolero" ("Oh, what unjust laws / to label me an outlaw").* In texts such as Ireneo Paz's novel *Vida y aventuras del más célebre bandido sonorense, Joaquín Murrieta* [*Life and Adventures of the most Celebrated Sonoran Bandit, Joaquín Murrieta*], published in Mexico City in 1904, the poem "Yo Soy Joaquín" ["I am Joaquín"] (1967) by the Chicano activist and poet Rodolfo "Corky" Gonzáles, and Pablo Neruda's play *Fulgor y Muerte de Joaquín Murieta* [*Splendor and Death of Joaquín Murieta*] (1967), Murieta emerges as a popular hero standing up against US racism and colonialism. Gonzáles's poem—which connects Murieta with other revolutionary figures from Mexican and Chicanx history—made the bandit an icon of the Chicano movement against economic and cultural imperialism in the 1960s: "our art, our literature, our music, they ignored / so they left the real things of value / and grabbed at their own destruction / by their greed and avarice. / They overlooked that cleansing fountain of / nature and brotherhood / which is Joaquín."†

Authors who have rewritten Ridge's *Joaquín Murrieta* for commercial and political purposes have frequently simplified the novel's cross-racial empathy and political complexities. The historical background of the Treaty of Guadalupe-Hidalgo and the displacement and disenfran-

---

* Unsigned, *Corrido de Joaquín Murrieta* recorded by the Sánchez and Linares Brothers in 1934, trans. Philip Sonnichsen et al. in Chris Strachwitz, ed. *Texas-Mexican Border Music*, vol. 2, Corridos Part 1: 1930–1934 (Folklyric Records, 1975).

† Gonzáles, *I am Joaquín /Yo Soy Joaquín: An Epic Poem by Rodolfo Gonzales with a Chronology of People and Events in Mexican and Mexican American History* (New York: Bantam, 1972).

chisement of many *Californios* is completely excised in the most popular manifestations of the Murieta legend. While Zorro—first introduced in Johnston McCulley's *The Curse of Capistrano* (1919)—echoes Murieta's romantic and chivalrous character and his vigilante methods, the pre-1846 setting of the Zorro stories makes Mexican rulers, rather than Americans, the agents of injustice.* Bob Kane, the creator of Batman, acknowledges Zorro as an important influence on Batman's vigilante persona,† but the Batman comics transform the masked vigilante into a member of the wealthy white elite. Whereas Zorro and Batman focus on redressing individual injustices, Ridge emphasizes Joaquín's network of fellow outlaws and their effort to avenge the US's racial injustices toward all Mexicans. In this trajectory of popular vigilante heroes, Ridge's Murieta becomes increasingly wealthy, white, and cut off from the social context of anti-Mexican racism.

That the seeds of such diverse (and often contradictory) interpretations and rewritings are contained in Ridge's brief, action-packed novel testifies to both Ridge's capacities as a writer and his political ambivalence as a writer of Cherokee descent who advocated for both disenfranchised *Californios* and the impartial rule of "sovereign law." The novel continually undermines Ridge's suggestion that the "pure administration" of the state government might put an end to "*injustice to individuals*" and "prejudice of color": If Mount Shasta symbolizes the impartial rule of law in Ridge's poem within the novel, we learn on the very next page that Murieta's outlaws hid themselves "in the rugged fastnesses" of the mountain. The novel concludes

---

* Curtis, *Zorro Unmasked: The Official History*, p. 75.

† Curtis, p. 22. For a discussion of Zorro and Batman as reworkings of the Murieta tradition, see Hausman, pp. 145–49.

with the grotesque exhibition throughout California of Murieta's severed head and Three-Fingered Jack's severed hand—a display intended to terrify would-be outlaws while publicizing the state's monopoly on violence. Although Ridge's novel did not result in the establishment of impartial laws, sensational stories about Mexican bandits certainly contributed to the justification of police powers in California. Just a year after *Joaquín Murieta*'s publication, California passed the Anti-Vagrancy Act, commonly known as the "Greaser Act," which targeted "all persons who are commonly known as 'Greasers' or the issue of Spanish and Indian blood . . . and who go armed and are not peaceable and quiet persons."

Joaquín Murieta is not just a foundational narrative of the state of California. It remains a vital novel today as racial profiling, deportations, criminalization, police violence, and racialized dispossession continue to devastate American communities in spite of putatively "colorblind" laws. Ridge's sympathetic account of Murieta's formation by unjust laws and racial violence offers a bracing rejoinder to racially disproportionate rates of incarceration, the systemic nature of antiblack police brutality, and the intensified militarization of the US-Mexico border fueled by racial stereotypes such as President Trump's invocation of "bad hombres." Through both its psychologically nuanced portrait of Murieta and the parallels it presents between him and the men authorized to enforce the law, Ridge's novel enjoins readers to reconsider US laws and their administration in connection with histories of racialization, dispossession, and state-sanctioned violence.

                                                    HSUAN L. HSU

Suggestions for Further Reading

Aleman, Jesse. "Assimilation and the Decapitated Body Politic in *The Life and Adventures of Joaquín Murieta.*" *Arizona Quarterly* 60:1 (Spring 2004), 71–98.

Christensen, Peter G. "Minority Interaction in John Rollin Ridge's *The Life and Adventures of Joaquín Murieta.*" *MELUS* 17:2 (Summer 1991–Summer 1992), 61–72.

Curtis, Sandra. *Zorro Unmasked: The Official History.* New York: Hyperion, 1998.

Donahue, Timothy. "Joaquín's Head: Theatrical Punishment, Public Address, and Novelistic Politics in the United States-Mexico Borderlands." *J19: The Journal of Nineteenth-Century Americanists* 4:2 (Fall 2016), 391–417.

Gonzáles, Rodolfo "Corky," *I am Joaquín / Yo Soy Joaquín: An Epic Poem by Rodolfo Gonzáles with a Chronology of People and Events in Mexican and Mexican American History.* New York: Bantam, 1972.

Hausman, Blake Michael. "Becoming Joaquin Murrieta: John Rollin Ridge and the Making of an Icon." PhD Dissertation. University of California, Berkeley, 2011.

Irwin, Robert. "Toward a Border Gnosis of the Borderlands: Joaquín Murrieta and Nineteenth-Century U.S.-Mexico Border Culture." *Nepantla: Views from the South* 2:3 (2001), 509–37.

Jackson, Joseph Henry. "Introduction." In *The Life and Adventures of Joaquín Murieta,* xi-l. Norman: University of Oklahoma Press, 1955.

Leal, Luis. "Introduction." Trans. Francisco Lamely and Miguel
    Lopez. In *Life and Adventures of the Celebrated Bandit Joa-
    quin Murieta, His Exploits in the State of California*, ix-cxiii.
    Ireneo Paz. Houston: Arte Público Press, 2001.

Madley, Benjamin. *An American Genocide: The United States
    and the California Indian Catastrophe, 1846–1873*. New
    Haven, CT: Yale University Press, 2016.

McWilliams, Carey. *California: The Great Exception*. Berkeley:
    University of California Press, 1999.

Owens, Louis. *Other Destinies: Understanding the American
    Indian Novel*. Norman: University of Oklahoma Press,
    1992.

Parins, James W. *John Rollin Ridge: His Life and Works*. Lincoln:
    University of Nebraska Press, 1991.

Ridge, John Rollin. *The Life and Adventures of Joaquin Murieta,
    the Celebrated California Bandit*. San Francisco: Frederick
    MacCrellish & Co., 1871.

_____. *Poems, by a Cherokee Indian, with an Account of the
    Assassination of His Father, John Ridge*. San Francisco:
    H. Payot, 1868.

_____. *A Trumpet of Our Own: Yellow Bird's Essays on the
    North American Indian: Selections from the Writings of the
    Noted Cherokee Author John Rollin Ridge*. Eds. David
    Farmer and Rennard Strickland. San Francisco: Book Club
    of California, 1981.

Rifkin, Mark. "'For the Wrongs of Our Poor Bleeding Country':
    Sensation, Class, and Empire in Ridge's *Joaquín Murieta*."
    Arizona Quarterly 65:2 (Summer 2009), 27–56.

Rodriguez, Richard. "The Head of Joaquín Murrieta." In *Days of
    Obligation: An Argument with My Mexican Father*, 133–148.
    New York: Penguin, 1992.

Rowe, John Carlos. "Highway Robbery: 'Indian Removal,' the
    Mexican-American War, and American Identity in 'The Life
    and Adventures of Joaquín Murieta.'" *NOVEL: A Forum on
    Fiction* 31:2 (Spring 1998), 149–73.

Smith, Caleb. "Crime Scenes: Fictions of Security in the Antebellum American Borderlands." In *Fatal Fictions: Crime and Investigation in Law and Literature*, 259–74. Eds. Alison L. LaCroix, Richard H. McAdams, and Martha C. Nussbaum. New York: Oxford University Press, 2016.

Stevens, Erica. "Three-Fingered Jack and the Severed Literary History of John Rollin Ridge's *The Life and Adventures of Joaquín Murieta*." *ESQ: A Journal of the American Renaissance* 61:1 (2015), 73–112.

Streeby, Shelley. "Joaquín Murieta and the American 1848." In *Post-Nationalist American Studies*, 166–96. Ed. John Carlos Rowe. Berkeley: University of California Press, 2000.

Unsigned, *Corrido de Joaquín Murrieta* recorded by the Sánchez and Linares Brothers in 1934, trans. Philip Sonnichsen et al. in Chris Strachwitz, ed. *Texas-Mexican Border Music*, vol. 2, Corridos Part 1: 1930–1934 (Folklyric Records, 1975).

Walker, Cheryl. *Indian Nation: Native American Literature and Nineteenth-Century Nationalisms*. Durham, NC: Duke University Press, 1997.

Whitley, Edward. "The First White Aboriginal: Walt Whitman and John Rollin Ridge." *ESQ: A Journal of the American Renaissance* 52:1–2 (2006), 105–39.

Windell, Maria. "Sanctify Our Suffering World with Tears: Transamerican Sentimentalism in *Joaquín Murieta*." *Nineteenth-Century Literature* 63:2 (Sept 2008), 170–96.

The Life and Adventures
of Joaquín Murieta

PUBLISHERS' PREFACE

The following production, aside from its intrinsic merit, will, no doubt, be read with increased interest when it is known that the author is a "Cherokee Indian," born in the woods—reared in the midst of the wildest scenery—and familiar with all that is thrilling, fearful, and tragical in a forest-life. His own experiences would seem to have well fitted him to portray in living colors the fearful scenes which are described in this book, connected as he was, from the age of seventeen up to twenty-three, with the tragical events which occurred so frequently in his own country, the rising of factions, the stormy controversies with the whites, the fall of distinguished chiefs, family feuds, individual retaliation and revenge, and all the consequences of that terrible civil commotion which followed the removal of the Cherokee Nation from the east to the west of the Mississippi, under the administration of Gen. Jackson. When a small boy, he saw his father (the celebrated chief and orator, known among the Indians by the name of "Sca-lee-los-kee") stabbed to death by a band of assassins employed by a political faction, in the presence of his wife and children at his own home. While the bleeding corpse of his father was yet lying in the house, surrounded by his weeping family, the news came that his grand-father, a distinguished old war-chief, was also killed; and, fast upon this report, that others of his near relatives were slain. His mother, a white woman and a native of Connecticut, fled from the bloody precincts of the nation, with her children, and sought refuge in the United States. Her oldest son, "Yellow Bird," after remaining several years among the whites, returned to his own country and asserted the rights of his family, which had been prostrated since the death of his father. He was intimately concerned for several years in the dangerous contentions which made the Cherokee Nation a place of blood; and, finally, not succeeding in overthrowing the murderers of his father and the oppressors of his country, who were then in power, and, having furnished them with a pretext for putting him out of the way by killing a prominent member of their party, he left his country once more and, in 1850, came to the State of California. So far, we know his history. Whether he will ever meet with success in his purposes with regard to his own people, we cannot say, but we hope that he will.

The perusal of this work will give those who are disposed to be curious an opportunity to estimate the character of Indian talent. The aboriginal race has produced great warriors, and powerful orators, but literary men— only a few.

EDITOR'S PREFACE

The Author, in presenting this book to the public, is aware that its chief merit consists in the reliability of the groundwork upon which it stands and not in the beauty of its composition. He has aimed to do a service—in his humble way—to those who shall hereafter inquire into the early history of California, by preserving, in however rude a shape, a record of at least a portion of those events which have made the early settlement of this State a living romance through all time.

Besides, it is but doing justice to a people who have so far degenerated as to have been called by many, "A Nation of Cowards," to hold up a manifest contradiction, or at least an exception to so sweeping an opinion, in the character of a man who, bad though he was, possessed a soul as full of unconquerable courage as ever belonged to a human being. Although the Mexicans may be whipped by every other nation, in a battle of two or five to one, yet no man who speaks the truth can ever deny that there lived one Mexican whose nerves were as iron in the face of danger and death.

The author has not thrown this work out into the world recklessly, or without authority for his assertions.

In the main, it will be found to be strictly true. Where he
has mentioned localities as being the harboring-places of
Joaquín, he has meant invariably to say that persons *then*
connected (at the date of the events narrated) with those
localities stood in the doubtful position in which he has
placed them.

JOAQUÍN MURIETA
The California Bandit

LIFE OF
JOAQUÍN MURIETA

I sit down to write somewhat concerning the life and character of *Joaquín Murieta*, a man as remarkable in the annals of crime as any of the renowned robbers of the Old or New World, who have preceded him; and I do this, not for the purpose of ministering to any depraved taste for the dark and horrible in human action, but rather to contribute my mite to those materials out of which the early history of California shall one day be composed. The character of this truly wonderful man was nothing more than a natural production of the social and moral condition of the country in which he lived, acting upon certain peculiar circumstances favorable to such a result, and, consequently, his individual history is a part of the most valuable history of the State.

There were two Joaquíns, bearing the various surnames of Murieta, O'Comorenia, Valenzuela, Botellier, and Carillo—so that it was supposed there were no less than five sanguinary devils ranging the country at one and the same time. It is now fully ascertained that there were only two, whose proper names were Joaquín Murieta and Joaquín Valenzuela, the latter being nothing more than a distinguished subordinate to the first, who is the Rinaldo Rinaldini[1] of California.

Joaquín Murieta was a Mexican, born in the province of Sonora of respectable parents and educated in the schools of Mexico. While growing up, he was remarkable for a very mild and peaceable disposition, and gave no sign of that indomitable and daring spirit which afterwards characterized him. Those who knew him in his school-boy days speak affectionately of his generous and noble nature at that period of his life and can scarcely credit the fact that the renowned and bloody bandit of California was one and the same being. At an early age of his manhood—indeed, while he was yet scarcely more than a boy—he became tired of the uncertain state of affairs in his own country, the usurpations and revolutions which were of such common occurrence, and resolved to try his fortunes among the American people, of whom he had formed the most favorable opinion from an acquaintance with the few whom he had met in his own native land. The war with Mexico[2] had been fought, and California belonged to the United States. Disgusted with the conduct of his degenerate countrymen and fired with enthusiastic admiration of the American character, the youthful Joaquín left his home with a buoyant heart and full of the exhilarating spirit of adventure. The first that we hear of him in the Golden State is that, in the spring of 1850, he is engaged in the honest occupation of a miner in the Stanislaus placers, then reckoned among the richest portions of the mines. He was then eighteen years of age, a little over the medium height, slenderly but gracefully built, and active as a young tiger. His complexion was neither very dark or very light, but clear and brilliant, and his countenance is pronounced to have been, at that time, exceedingly handsome and attractive. His large black eyes, kindling with the enthusiasm of his earnest nature, his firm and well-formed mouth, his well-shaped head from which the long, glossy, black hair hung down over his shoulders, his silvery voice full of generous utterance, and the frank and cordial bearing which distinguished him made him beloved by all with whom he came in contact. He had the confidence and respect of the whole community around him, and was fast amassing a fortune from his rich mining claim. He had built him a comfortable mining residence in which he had domiciled his heart's treasure—a beautiful Sonorian girl, who had followed the young adventure in all his wanderings with that devotedness of passion which belongs to the dark-eyed damsels of Mexico. It was at this moment of peace and felicity that a blight came over the young man's prospects. The country was then full of lawless and desperate men, who bore the name of Americans but failed to support the honor and dignity of that title. A feeling was prevalent among this class of contempt for any and all Mexicans, whom they looked upon as no better than conquered subjects of the United States, having no rights which could stand before a haughtier and superior race. They made no exceptions. If the proud blood of the Castilians[3] mounted to the cheek of a partial descendant of the Mexiques,[4] showing that he had inherited the old chivalrous spirit of his Spanish ancestry, they looked upon it as a saucy presumption in one so inferior to them. The prejudice of color, the antipathy of races, which are always stronger and bitterer with the ignorant and unlettered, they could not overcome, or if they could, would not, because it afforded them a convenient excuse for their unmanly cruelty and oppression. A band of these lawless men, having the brute power to do as they pleased, visited Joaquín's house and peremptorily bade him leave his claim, as they would allow no Mexicans to work in that region. Upon his remonstrating against such outrageous conduct, they struck him violently over the face, and, being physically superior, compelled him to swallow his wrath. Not content with this, they tied him hand and foot and ravished his mistress before his eyes. They left him, but the soul of the young man was from that moment darkened. It was the first injury he had ever received at the hands of the Americans, whom he had always hitherto respected, and it wrung him to the soul as a deeper and deadlier wrong from that very circumstance. He departed with his weeping and almost heartbroken mistress for a more northern portion of the mines; and the next we hear of him, he is cultivating a little farm on the banks of a beautiful stream that watered a fertile valley, far out in the seclusion of the mountains. Here he might hope for peace—here he might forget the past, and again be happy. But his dream was not destined to last. A company of unprincipled Americans—shame that there should be such bearing the name!—saw his retreat, coveted his little home surrounded by its fertile tract of land, and drove him from it, with no other excuse than that he was "an infernal Mexican intruder!" Joaquín's blood boiled in his veins, but his spirit was still unbroken, nor had the iron so far entered his soul as to sear up the innate sensitiveness to honor and right which reigned in his bosom. Twice broken up in his honest pursuit of fortune, he resolved still to labor on with unflinching brow and with that true *moral* bravery, which throws its redeeming light forward upon his subsequently dark and criminal career. How deep must have been the anguish of that young heart and how strongly rooted the native honesty of his soul, none can know or imagine but they who have been tried in a like manner. He bundled up his little movable property, still accompanied by his faithful bosom-friend, and again started forth to strike once more, like a brave and honest man, for fortune and for happiness. He arrived at "Murphy's Diggings" in Calaveras County, in the month of April, and went again to mining, but, meeting with nothing like his former success, he soon abandoned that business and devoted his time to dealing "monte," a game which is common in Mexico, and has been almost universally adopted by gamblers in California. It is considered by the Mexican in no manner a disreputable employment, and many well-raised young men from the Atlantic States have resorted to it as a profession in this land of luck and chances. It was then in much better odor than it is now, although it is at present a game which may be played on very fair and honest principles; provided, anything can be strictly honest or fair which allows the taking of money without a valuable consideration. It was therefore looked upon as no departure from rectitude on the part of Joaquín, when he commenced the business of dealing "monte."[5] Having a very pleasing exterior and being, despite of all his sorrows, very gay and lively in disposition, he attracted many persons to his table, and won their money with such skill and grace, or lost his own with such perfect good humor that he was considered by all the very beau ideal of a gambler and the prince of clever fellows. His sky seemed clear and his prospects bright, but Fate was weaving her mysterious web around him, and fitting him to be by the force of circumstances what nature never intended to make him.

He had gone a short distance from Murphy's Diggings to see a half-brother, who had been located in that vicinity for several months, and returned to Murphy's upon a horse which his brother had lent him. The animal proved to have been stolen, and being recognized by a number of individuals in town, an excitement was raised on the subject. Joaquín suddenly found himself surrounded by a furious mob and charged with the crime of theft. He told them how it happened that he was riding the horse and in what manner his half-brother had come in possession of it. They listened to no explanation, but bound him to a tree, and publicly disgraced him with the lash. They then proceeded to the house of his half-brother and hung him without judge or jury. It was then that the character of Joaquín changed, suddenly and irrevocably. Wanton cruelty and the tyranny of prejudice had reached their climax. His soul swelled beyond its former boundaries, and the barriers of honor, rocked into atoms by the strong passion which shook his heart like an earthquake, crumbled around him. Then it was that he declared to a friend that he would live henceforth for revenge and that his path should be marked with blood. Fearfully did he keep his promise, as the following pages will show.

It was not long after this unfortunate affair that an American was found dead in the vicinity of Murphy's Diggings, having been cut to pieces with a knife. Though horribly mangled, he was recognized as one of the mob engaged in whipping Joaquín. A doctor, passing in the neighborhood of this murder, was met, shortly afterward, by two men on horseback, who fired their revolvers at him, but, owing to his speed on foot, and the unevenness of the ground, he succeeded in escaping with no further injury than having a bullet shot through his hat within an inch of the top of his head! A panic spread among the rash individuals who had composed that mob, and they were afraid to stir out on their ordinary business. Whenever any one of them strayed out of sight of his camp or ventured to travel on the highway, he was shot down suddenly and mysteriously. Report after report came into the villages that Americans had been found dead on the highways, having been either shot or stabbed, and it was invariably discovered, for many weeks, that the murdered men belonged to the mob who publicly whipped Joaquín. It was fearful and it was strange to see how swiftly and mysteriously those men disappeared. "Murieta's revenge was very nearly complete," said an eyewitness of these events, in reply to an inquiry which I addressed him. "I am inclined to think he *wiped out* the most of those prominently engaged in whipping him."

Thus far, who can blame him? But the iron had entered too deeply in his soul for him to stop here. He had contracted a hatred to the whole American race, and was determined to shed their blood, whenever and wherever an opportunity occurred. It was no time now for him to retrace his steps. He had committed deeds which made him amenable to the law, and his only safety lay in a persistence in the unlawful course which he had begun. It was necessary that he should have horses and that he should have money. These he could not obtain except by robbery and murder, and thus he became an outlaw and a bandit on the verge of his nineteenth year.

The year 1850 rolled away, marked with the eventful history of this young man's wrongs and trials, his bitter revenge on those who had perpetrated the crowning act of his deep injury and disgrace; and, as it closed, it shut him away forever from his peace of mind and purity of heart. He walked forth into the future a dark, determined criminal, and his proud nobility of soul existed only in memory.

It became generally known in 1851 that an organized banditti was ranging the country; but it was not yet ascertained who was the leader. Travelers, laden with the produce of the mines, were met upon the roads by well-dressed men who politely invited them to "stand and deliver"; persons riding alone in the many wild and lonesome regions, which form a large portion of this country, were skillfully noosed with the lasso (which the Mexicans throw with great accuracy, being able thus to capture wild cattle, elk, and sometimes even grizzly bears, upon the plains), dragged from their saddles, and murdered in the adjacent thickets. Horses of the finest mettle were stolen from the ranches, and, being tracked up, were found in the possession of a determined band of men, ready to retain them at all hazards and fully able to stand their ground. The scenes of murder and robbery shifted with the rapidity of lightning. At one time, the northern countries would be suffering slaughters and depredations, at another the southern, and, before one would have imagined it possible, the east and the west, and every point of the compass would be in trouble. There had never been before this, either in '49 or '50, any such as an organized banditti, and it had been a matter of surprise to every one, since the country was so well adapted to a business of this kind— the houses scattered at such distances along the roads, the plains so level and open in which to ride with speed, and the mountains so rugged with their ten thousand fastnesses in which to hide. Grass was abundant in the far-off valleys which lay hidden in the rocky gorges, cool, delicious streams made music at the feet of the towering peaks, or came leaping down in gladness from their sides—game abounded on every hand, and nine unclouded months of the year made a climate so salubrious that nothing could be sweeter than a day's rest under the tall pines or a night's repose under the open canopy of Heaven. Joaquín knew his advantages. His superior intelligence and education gave him the respect of his comrades, and, appealing to the prejudice against the "Yankees," which the disastrous results of the Mexican war had not tended to lessen in their minds, he soon assembled around him a powerful band of his countrymen, who daily increased, as he ran his career of almost magical success. Among the number was Manuel Garcia, more frequently known as "Three-Fingered Jack," from the fact of his having had one of his fingers shot off in a skirmish with an American party during the Mexican war. He was a man of unflinching bravery, but cruel and sanguinary. His form was large and rugged and his countenance so fierce that few liked to look upon it. He was different from his more youthful leader, in possessing nothing of his generous, frank, and cordial disposition, and in being utterly destitute of one merciful trait of humanity. His delight was in murder for its own diabolical sake, and he gloated over the agonies of his unoffending victims. He would sacrifice policy, the safety and interests of the band for the mere gratification of this murderous propensity, and it required all Joaquín's firmness and determination to hold him in check. The history of this monster was well known before he joined Joaquín. He was known to be the same man, who, in 1846, surrounded with his party two Americans, young men by the name of Cowie and Fowler, as they were traveling on the road between Sonoma and Bodega, stripped them entirely naked, and, binding them each to a tree, slowly tortured them to death. He began by throwing knives at their bodies, as if he were practicing at a target; he then cut out their tongues, punched out their eyes with his knife, gashed their bodies in numerous places, and, finally, flaying them alive, left them to die. A thousand cruelties like these had he been guilty of, and, long before Joaquín knew him, he was a hardened experienced, and detestable monster. When it was necessary for the young chief to commit some peculiarly horrible and cold-blooded murder, some deed of hellish ghastliness at which his soul revolted, he deputed this man to do it. And well was it executed, with certainty and to the letter.

Another member of this band was Reyes Feliz, a youth of sixteen years of age, who had read the wild romantic lives of the chivalrous robbers of Spain and Mexico until his enthusiastic spirit had become imbued with the same sentiments which actuated them, and he could conceive of nothing grander than to throw himself back upon the strictly natural rights of man and hurl defiance at society and its laws. He also was a Sonorian, and the beautiful mistress of Joaquín was his sister. He was a devoted follower of his chief; like him, brave, impulsive, and generous.

A third member was Claudio, a man about thirty-five years of age, of lean but vigorous constitution, a dark complexion, and possessing a somewhat savage but lively and expressive countenance. He was indisputably brave, but exceedingly cautious and cunning, springing upon his prey at an unexpected moment and executing his purposes with the greatest possible secrecy as well as precision. He was a deep calculator, a wily schemer, and could wear the appearance of an honest man with the same grace and ease that he would show in throwing around his commanding figure the magnificent cloak in which he prided. In disposition, he was revengeful, tenacious in his memory of a wrong, sly and secret in his windings as a serpent, and, with less nobility than the rattlesnake, he gave no warning before he struck. Yet, as I have said before, he was brave when occasion called it forth, and, although ever ready to take an advantage, he never flinched in the presence of danger. This extreme caution, united with a strong will and the courage to do, made him an exceedingly formidable man.

A fourth member was Joaquín Valenzuela, who has been frequently confounded with Joaquín Murieta, from the fact that the latter threw upon him much responsibility in the government of the band and entrusted him with important expeditions, requiring in their execution a great amount of skill and experience. Valenzuela was a much older man than his leader, and had acted for many years in Mexico as a bandit under the famous guerilla chief, Padre Jurata.[6]

Another distinguished member was Pedro Gonzalez, less brave than many others, but a skillful spy and expert horse-thief, and as such, an invaluable adjunct to a company of mounted men, who required a continual supply of fresh horses as well as a thorough knowledge of the state of affairs around them.

There were many others belonging to this organization whom it is not necessary to describe. It is sufficient to say that they composed as formidable a force of outlaws as ever gladdened the eye of an acknowledged leader. Their number, at this early period, is not accurately known, but a fair estimate would not place it at a lower figure than fifty, with the advantage of a continual and steady increase.

Such was the unsettled condition of things, so distant and isolated were the different mining regions, so lonely and uninhabited the sections through which the roads and trails were cut, and so numerous the friends and acquaintances of the bandits themselves that these lawless men carried on their operations with almost absolute impunity. It was a rule with them to injure no man who ever extended them a favor, and, whilst they plundered every one else and spread devastation in every other quarter, they invariably left those ranches and houses unharmed whose owners and inmates had afforded them shelter or assistance. Many persons, who were otherwise honestly inclined, bought the safety of their lives and property by remaining scrupulously silent in regard to Joaquín and neutral in every attempt to do him an injury. Further than this, there were many large rancheros[7] who were secretly connected with the banditti, and stood ready to harbor them in times of danger and to furnish them with the best animals that fed on their extensive pastures. The names of several of these wealthy and highly respectable individuals are well known, and will transpire in the course of this history.

At the head of this most powerful combination of men, Joaquín ravaged the State in various quarters during the

year 1851, without at that time being generally known as
the leader; his subordinates, Claudio, Valenzuela, and
Pedro Gonzalez being alternately mistaken for the actual
chief. Except to few persons, even his name was unknown, and many were personally acquainted with him
and frequently saw him in the different towns and villages, without having the remotest idea that he stood
connected with the bloody events which were then filling
the country with terror and dismay. He resided for weeks
at a time in different localities, ostensibly engaged in
gambling, or employed as a vaquero, a packer, or in some
other apparently honest avocation, spending much of his
time in the society of that sweetest of all companions the
woman that he loved.

While living in a secluded part of the town of San José,
sometime in the summer of '51, he one night became violently engaged in a row at a fandango,[8] was arrested for a
breach of the peace, brought up before a magistrate, and
fined twelve dollars. He was in the charge of Mr. Clark,
the deputy sheriff of Santa Clara County, who had made
himself particularly obnoxious to the banditti by his rig-
orous scrutiny into their conduct and his determined attempts to arrest some of their number. Joaquín had the
complete advantage of him, inasmuch as the deputy was
totally ignorant of the true character of the man with
whom he had to deal. With the utmost frankness in his
manner, Joaquín requested him to walk down to his residence in the skirts of the town, and he would pay him the
money. They proceeded together, engaged in a pleasant
conversation, until they reached the edge of a thicket
when the young bandit suddenly drew a knife and informed Clark that he had brought him there to kill him,
at the same instant stabbing him to the heart before he
could draw his revolver. Though many persons knew the
author of this most cool and bloody deed by sight, yet it

was a long time before it was ascertained that the escaped murderer was no less a personage than the leader of the daring cut-throats who were then infesting the country.

In the fall of the same year, Joaquín moved up in the more northern part of the State and settled himself down with his mistress at the Sonorian Camp, a cluster of tents and cloth houses situated about three miles from the city of Marysville, in Yuba County. It was not long before the entire country rung with the accounts of frequent, startling, and diabolical murders. *The Marysville Herald* of November 13, 1851, speaking of the horrible state of affairs, has the following remarkable paragraph:

"Seven men have been murdered within three or four days in a region of country not more than twelve miles in extent."

Shortly after the murders thus mentioned, two men who were traveling on the road that leads up Feather River, near to the Honcut Creek, which puts into that stream, discovered just ahead of them four Mexicans, one of whom was dragging at his saddlebow by a lariat an American whom they had just lassoed around the neck. The two travelers did not think it prudent to interfere, and so hurried on to a place of safety, and reported what they had seen. Legal search being made upon this information, six other men were found murdered near the same place, bearing upon their throats the fatal mark of the lariat.

Close upon these outrages, reports came that several individuals had been killed and robbed at Bidwel's Bar, some ten or fifteen miles up the river. Consternation spread like fire—fear thrilled through the hearts of hundreds, and all dreaded to travel the public roads.

Suspicion was directed to the Sonorian Camp, it being occupied exclusively by Mexicans, many of whom had no ostensible employment, and yet rode fine horses and spent

money freely. This suspicion was confirmed by a partial
confession obtained from a Mexican thief who had fallen
into the hands of the "Vigilance Committee" of Marysville and had been run up with a rope several times to the
limb of a tree, by order of that formidable body. The
sheriff of Yuba County, R. B. Buchanan, went out on a
moonlight night with his *posse* (which, to say the truth,
consisted of one man only, widely and familiarly known
as Ike Bowen) to examine the premises and to arrest three
suspicious characters, who were known to be lurking in
that neighborhood. While getting through the bars of a
fence, they were attacked from behind by three Mexicans
who had been hid, and the sheriff was severely wounded
with a pistol-ball, which struck him near the spine, and
passing through his body, came out in the front near the
navel. The Mexicans escaped, and Buchanan was finally
taken back to Marysville, where he lay a long time in a
very dangerous situation but eventually recovered much
to the gratification of the community, who admired the
devotion and courage with which he had well-nigh sacri-
ficed his life in the discharge of his duties. He, in common with every one else, was, for a long time afterward,
in ignorance that he had received his wound in a personal
encounter with the redoubtable Joaquín himself.

The bandits did not remain long in the vicinity of
Marysville after this occurrence but rode off into the
coast range of mountains to the west of Mount Shasta, a
conspicuous land-mark in the northern portion of the
State, which rears its white shaft at all seasons of the year
high above every other peak, and serves at a distance of
two hundred miles to direct the course of the mountain-
traveler, being to him as the polar star to the mariner.
Gazing at it from the Sacramento Valley at a distance of
one hundred and fifty miles, it rises in its garments of

snow like some mighty archangel, filling the Heaven with his solemn presence.

MOUNT SHASTA, SEEN FROM A DISTANCE*

Behold the dread Mount Shasta, where it stands,
Imperial midst the lesser hight, and like
Some mighty, unimpassioned mind, companionless
And cold. The storms of Heaven may beat in wrath
Against it, but it stands in unpoluted
Grandeur still; and from the rolling mists up-heaves
Its tower of pride e'en purer than before.
Each wintry shower, and white-winged tempest leave
Their frozen tributes on its brow, and it
Doth make of them an everlasting crown.
Thus doth it day by day, and age by age,
Defy each stroke of time—still rising higher
Into Heaven!

Aspiring to the eagle's cloudless hight,
No human foot hath stained its snowy side,
Nor human breath has dimmed the icy mirror
Which it holds unto the moon, and stars, and sov'reign
Sun. We may not grow familiar with the secrets
Of its hoary top, whereon the Genius
Of that mountain builds his glorious throne!
Far-lifted in the boundless blue, he doth
Encircle, with his gaze supreme, the broad
Dominions of the West, that lie beneath
His feet, in pictures of sublime repose
No artist ever drew. He sees the tall,
Gigantic hills arise in silentness

* Written by "YELLOW BIRD," in 1852.

And peace, and in the long review of distance
Range themselves in order grand. He sees the sunlight
Play upon the golden streams that through the valleys
Glide. He hears the music of the great and solemn
Sea, and over-looks the huge old western wall,
To view the birth-place of undying Melody!

Itself all light, save when some loftiest cloud
Doth for a while embrace its cold forbidding
Form—that monarch-mountain casts its mighty
Shadows down upon the crownless peaks below,
That, like inferior minds to some great
Spirit, stand in strong contrasted littleness!
All through the long and summery months of our
Most tranquil year, it points its icy shaft
On high, to catch the dazzling beams that fall
In showers of splendor round that crystal cone,
And roll, in floods of far magnificence,
Away from that lone vast Reflector in
The dome of Heaven.

Still watchful of the fertile
Vale, and undulating plains below, the grass
Grows greener in its shade, and sweeter bloom
The flowers. Strong Purifier! From its snowy
Side the breezes cool are wafted to "the peaceful
Homes of men,"⁹ who shelter at its feet, and love
To gaze upon its honored form; aye, standing
There, the guarantee of health and happiness!
Well might it win communities so blest
To loftier feelings, and to nobler thoughts—
The great material symbol of eternal
Things! And well, I ween, in after years, how,
In the middle of his furrowed track, the plowman,
In some sultry hour, will pause, and, wiping

From his brow the dusty sweat, with reverence
Gaze upon that hoary peak. The herdsman
Oft will rein his charger in the plain, and drink
Into his inmost soul the calm sublimity;
And little children, playing on the green, shall
Cease their sport, and, turning to that mountain
Old, shall, of their mother ask, "Who made it?"
And she shall answer, "God!"
And well this Golden State shall thrive, if, like
Its own Mount Shasta, sovereign law shall lift
Itself in purer atmosphere—so high
That human feeling, human passion, at its base
Shall lie subdued; e'en pity's tears shall on
Its summit freeze; to warm it, e'en the sunlight
Of deep sympathy shall fail—
Its pure administration shall be like
The snow, immaculate upon that mountain's brow!

In the rugged fastnesses of the wild range lying to the west of this huge mount, a range inhabited only by human savages and savage beasts, did the outlaws hide themselves for several long months, descending into the valleys at intervals with no further purpose than to steal horses, of which they seemed determined to keep a good supply. They induced the Indians to aid them in this *laudable* purpose, and so efficiently did these simple people render their assistance that the rancheros of that region loaded the very air with their curses of the "naked devils," who tormented them to such an intolerable degree! On one occasion, during these depredations upon locomotive property, an exasperated party of Americans, who had been on track of their stolen animals, came up with the Indian thieves and managed to hem them between a perpendicular wall of bluffs and a deep river, so that there was no escape for them but to swim the stream, which swept by in a mad and foaming torrent. They fired upon the Indians, who leaped into the water, many of them dyeing it with their blood, and a few successfully swimming across. In the midst of the firing, a tall Mexican, mounted upon a fine horse, dashed down the banks, firing his revolver as he went, and plunged into the stream. His horse struck boldly with him for the opposite shore, and he had gained the middle of the current a distance of a hundred yards from his pursuers, before any effectual shot at him was made. He was about to escape, and nothing would now avail but a dead aim and a steady nerve. The best marksman in the crowd, a lank Missourian, dismounted from his horse, drew his rifle to his shoulder while the others looked anxiously on, and taking a long "bead," fired. The Mexican leaned forward a moment, and the next instant floated from the saddle and sunk, while his fine charger breasted the waves and ascended the bank with a snorting nostril and dripping mane. No one was willing to risk the dangerous passage even to possess so noble an animal, and they returned with their recovered property to their homes. This tall Mexican was, without doubt, a member of Joaquín's band, who had led the Indians in that very unsuccessful thieving expedition.

In that desolate region, through which, at long intervals, only a few straggling miners passed on their lonesome prospecting tours, human skeletons were found bleaching in the sun, some leaving no trace of the manner in which they perished, while others plainly showed by the perforated skull that the leaden ball had suddenly and secretly done its work. The ignorant Indians suffered for many a deed which had been perpetrated by civilized hands. It will be recollected by many persons who resided at Yreka and on Scott's River in the fall and winter of 1851 how many "prospecters" were lost in the mountains and never again heard from; how many were found dead, supposed to have been killed by the Indians, and yet bearing upon their bodies the marks of knives and bullets quite as frequently as arrows.

As soon as the spring opened in 1852, Joaquín and his party descended from the mountains, and, by forced marches in the night, drove some two or three hundred horses which they had collected at their winter rendez-vous down through the southern portion of the State into the province of Sonora. Returning in a few weeks, they took up their head-quarters at Arroyo Cantoova,[10] a fine tract of rich pasturage, containing seven or eight thousand acres, beautifully watered, and fenced in by a circular wall of mountains through which an entrance was afforded by a narrow gate or pass, at which a very formidable force could be stayed in their progress by a small body of men. This rich and fertile basin lies half-way between the Tejon and the Pacheco Pass, to the east of the coast range and to the west of the great Tulare Lake, thoroughly embosomed in its rugged boundaries and the more valuable as a retreat that it was distant at least one hundred and fifty miles from any human habitation. From the surrounding eminences, an approaching enemy could be seen for a long way off. This region was, in one respect in particular, adapted to the purpose for which it was chosen, and that is, it abounded in game of every kind: elk, antelope, deer, grizzly bears, quails, grouse, and every species of smaller animals most desirable for food. Here Joaquín selected a clump of evergreen oaks for his residence, and many a pleasant day found him and his still blooming companion roofed by the rich foliage of the trees and reclining upon a more luxurious carpet than ever blossomed, with its imitative flowers, beneath the satin-slippered feet of the fairest daughters of San Francisco. The brow of his sweet and faithful friend would sometimes grow sad as she recurred to the happy and peaceful lives which they had once lived, but with a woman's true nature, she loved him in spite of all his crimes, and her soul was again lighted up as she gazed into those dark and glorious eyes which had never quailed before mortal man, and lost their fierceness only when they looked on her. Besides, in her tender heart she made for him many allowances; she saw many strong palliations of his conduct in the treatment which he had received—she knew the secret history of his soul, his sufferings, and his struggles with an evil fate, and the long agony which rent up by the roots the original honesty of his high-born nature. More than this, he had told her that he would soon finish his dangerous career, when, having completed his revenge, and, having accumulated an equivalent for the fortune of which he had been robbed by the Americans, he would retire into a peaceful portion of the State of Sonora, build him a pleasant home, and live alone for love and her. She believed him, for he spoke truly of his intentions, and wonder not, ye denizens of cities! she was happy even in the wilderness. It matter not how the world regarded him, to her he was all that is noble, generous, and beautiful.

After spending a few weeks at the rendezvous, Joaquín divided his party, then consisting of about seventy men, into different bands headed by Claudio, Three-Fingered Jack, and Valenzuela, and dispatched them to various quarters with orders to devote themselves chiefly to stealing horses and mules, as he had a purpose to effect which required at least fifteen hundred or two thousand animals. He himself started on a separate course, accompanied by Reyes Feliz, Pedro Gonzalez, and Juan. Three females, who were dressed in male attire and well armed, were also in company; that is to say Joaquín's mistress, and the wives of Reyes Feliz and Pedro Gonzalez. All the party were well mounted, and rode, no one knew whither, except Joaquín himself. Arriving at Mokelumne Hill in Calaveras County, they took up quarters with some of their Mexican acquaintances in that place, and, passing through the streets, or visiting the saloons, were looked upon as nothing more than peaceable Mexicans, residing in the town. This was in the month of April. While here, the women appeared in their proper attire, and were admired for their exceedingly modest and quiet deportment. The men issued forth at night upon no praiseworthy missions, and, mounted upon their magnificent chargers, scoured an extent of many miles ere they returned stealthily back to their hiding place and the arms of their languishing loves. Joaquín bore the appearance and character of an elegant and successful gambler, being amply provided with means from his night excursions.

In the meantime his men were, in different directions, prosecuting with ardor the business upon which they had been sent, and there was a universal cry throughout the lower country that horse-thieves were very nearly impoverishing the ranchos. Joaquín gathered a pretty good knowledge of what his followers were about from the newspapers, which made a very free use of his own name in the accounts of these transactions and handled his character in no measured terms. In the various outbreaks in which he had been personally engaged, he had worn different disguises, and was actually disguised the most when he showed his real features. No man who had met him on the highway would be apt to recognize him in the cities. He frequently stood very unconcernedly in a crowd, and listened to long and earnest conversations in relation to himself, and laughed in his sleeve at the many conjectures which were made as to his whereabouts and intentions.

After remaining as long as he desired at Mokelumne Hill, about the first of May he prepared to take his

departure, which he resolved to do at the hour of midnight. His horses were saddled, the women dressed in
their male clothes, and everything ready, when Joaquín
sauntered out into the streets, according to his custom,
and visited the various drinking and gambling saloons,
with which every California town and village abound.
While sitting at a monte table, at which he carelessly put
down a dollar or two to while away the time, his attention was suddenly arrested by the distinct pronunciation
of his name just opposite to where he sat. Looking up, he
observed three or four Americans engaged in loud and
earnest conversation in relation to his identical self, in
which one of them, a tall fellow armed with a revolver,
remarked that he "would just like once in his life to come
across Joaquín, and that he would kill him as quick as he
would a snake." The daring bandit, upon hearing this
speech, jumped on the monte table in view of the whole
house, and, drawing his sixshooter, shouted out, "I am
Joaquín! if there is any shooting to do, I am in." So sudden and startling was this movement that every one
quailed before him, and, in the midst of the consternation and confusion which reigned, he gathered his cloak
about him and walked out unharmed. After this bold
avowal of himself, it was necessary for him to make his
stay quite short in that vicinity. Mounting his horse,
therefore, with expedition, he dashed off with his party
at his heels, sending back a whoop of defiance which
rung out thrillingly upon the night air. The extreme cha-
grin of the citizens can be imagined when they found, for
the first time, that they had unwittingly tolerated in their
very midst the man whom, above all others, they would
have wished to get hold of.

Returning to his rendezvous at Arroyo Cantoova, he
found that his marauding bands had collected some two
or three hundred head of horses, and were patiently

waiting his further orders. He detached a portion of them to take the animals into Sonora for safe keeping and made remittances of money at the same time to a secret partner of his in that State.

Towards the last of May, becoming again restless and tired of an inactive life, he started forth upon the high-roads, attended as before, when on his visit to Moke-lumne Hill, simply by Reyes Feliz, Pedro Gonzalez, Juan, and the three bright-eyed girls, who, mounted on very elegant chargers, appeared as charming a trio of hand-some cavaliers as ever delighted the visions of romantic damsels. Meeting with no one for a week or two but im-poverished Frenchmen and dilapidated Germans in search of "diggings," and having sent very nearly all his money to Sonora, Joaquín's purse was getting pretty low, and he resolved to attack the first man or men he might meet, who appeared to be supplied. He was at this time on the road to San Luis Gonzagos, to which place a young American, named Allen Ruddle, was at the same time driving a wagon, loaded with groceries. Overtaking this young man on an open plain, Joaquín, leaving his party behind, rode up to him where he sat on one of his wheel-horses, and, politely bidding him "good morning," requested of him the loan of what small change he might have about him, remarking at the same moment:

"It is true, I am a robber, but, as sure as I live, I merely wish to *borrow* this money, and I will as certainly pay it back to you as my name is Joaquín. It is not often that I am without funds, but such is my situation at present."

Ruddle, without replying, made a sudden motion to draw his pistol, upon which Joaquín exclaimed:

"Come, don't be foolish—I have no wish to kill you, and let us have no fight."

Ruddle made another effort to get his pistol, which, from excitement, or perhaps from its hanging in the holster, he could not instantly draw, when the bandit, with a muttered oath, slashed him across the neck with his bowie-knife and dashed him from the saddle. Searching his pockets, he found about three hundred dollars. His party coming up, he rode on, leaving the murdered man where he lay and his wagon and team standing by the road. Joaquín's conscience smote him for this deed, and he regretted the necessity of killing so honest and hard-working a man as Ruddle seemed to be.

It happened that just at this period, Capt. Harry Love, whose own history is one of equal romance with that of Joaquín but marked only with events which redound to his honor, was at the head of a small party gotten up on his own responsibility in search of this outrageous bandit. Love had served as an express rider[11] in the Mexican war and had borne dispatches from one military post to another over the most dangerous tracts of Mexico. He had traveled alone for hundreds of miles over mountains and deserts, beset with no less danger than the dreaded "guerillas" who hung upon the skirts of the American army, laid-in-wait at mountain-passes and watering-places, and made it their business to murder every unfortunate straggler that fell into their hands. Riding fleet horses and expert in the use of the lasso, it required a well-mounted horseman to escape them on the open plains, and many a hard race with them has the Captain had to save his neck and the valuable papers in his charge. He had been, moreover, from his early youth, a hardy pioneer, experienced in all the dangers and hardships of a border-life. Having these antecedents in his favor and possessing the utmost coolness in the presence of danger, he was a man well-fitted to contend with a person like Joaquín, than whom the lightning was not quicker and surer in the execution of a deadly errand. Love was on the direct trail of Joaquín when Ruddle was murdered.

With the utmost speed consistent with the caution necessary to a surprise of the bandit, he pursued him by his murders and robberies which left a bloody trail behind him to the rancho of San Luis Gonzagos, which is now well known to have been a place which regularly harbored the banditti. Arriving at that place at night, he ascertained by certain spies whom he had employed that the party of whom he was in search were staying in a canvas-house on the edge of the rancho.

Proceeding cautiously to this house with his men, the Captain had just reached the door when the alarm was given by a woman in a neighboring tent, and, in an instant, Joaquín, Gonzalez, Reyes Feliz, and Juan had cut their way through the back part and escaped into the darkness. Upon entering, no one was to be seen but women, three of whom, then dressed in their proper garments, were the bandits' mistresses, of which fact, however, Love was ignorant. Leaving the women to shift for themselves, the fugitives went to their horses, which were hitched in an adjacent thicket, mounted them, and rode directly over to Oris Timbers, a distance of eight miles, where they immediately stole twenty head of horses and drove them off into the neighboring mountains. They remained concealed all the next day but at night came back (a movement wholly unanticipated by Love) to the cloth-house where they had left their women, who quickly doffed their female attire and rode off with their companions into the hills, from which they had just come. Driving the stolen horses before them, the party started in high glee across the Tulare Plains for Los Angeles. Love followed them no further, having business which re-called him. The owner of the Oris Timbers Rancho, however, attended by a few Americans, fell upon their trail, indicated by the Captain, and pursued them without much difficulty into the country of the Tejon Indians.[12] Not

coming up with them, and perhaps not very anxious to do
so, the owner of the horses proceeded with his attendants
to the seat of government of the Tejon Nation in order to
see the old chief, Sapatarra,[13] and, if possible, to make an
arrangement with him by which to recover his property.
They soon reached the capital, which consisted of twenty
or thirty very picturesque-looking bark huts scattered
along the side of a hill, in front of the largest of which
they found old Sapatarra, seated upon his haunches in all
the grandeur of "naked majesty," enjoying a very luxurious repast of roasted acorns and dried angle-worms. His
swarthy subjects were scattered in various directions
around him, engaged for the most part in the very ardu-
ous task of doing nothing. The little smoky-looking children were sporting, like a black species of water-fowl, in
the creek which ran a short distance below while the
women were pounding with stone pestles in stone mor-
tars, industriously preparing their acorn bread. The deli-
cacies of the chief's table were soon spread before his
guests, which, though tempting, they respectfully declined
and entered immediately upon their business. Sapatarra
was informed that a party of Mexican horse-thieves had
sought shelter in his boundaries; that they were only a few
in number, and that they had in their possession twenty
splendid horses, one-half of which should belong to the
chief if he recovered the whole number. This arrangement
was speedily effected, and the high contracting parties
separated with great satisfaction and mutual assurances
of their distinguished regard.

Sapatarra held a council of state, which resulted in
sending spies over his dominions to discover traces of the
marauding band. Information was returned in a day or
two that seven Mexicanos, superbly dressed, and covered
with splendid jewelry, and having a large number of fine
horses, were camped on a little stream about fifteen miles

from the capital. The cupidity of the old chief and his right-hand men was raised to the highest pitch, and they resolved to manage the matter in hand with great skill and caution; which last, by the way, is a quality that particularly distinguishes the California Indians, amounting to so extreme a degree that it might safely be called cowardice. Joaquín and party, having ascertained that they were no longer pursued by the Oris Timbers Ranchero, and feeling perfectly secure amongst so harmless a people as the Tejons, disencumbered themselves of their weapons and resolved to spend a few days in careless repose and genuine rural enjoyment. Juan was, one evening, lying in the grass, watching the horses as they fed around him, while Gonzalez, Feliz, and Murieta were each of them separately seated under a live-oak tree, enjoying a private *tête-à-tête*[14] with their beloved and loving partners. The evening shades were softly stealing around them, and all nature seemed to lull their unquiet spirits to security and repose. Just at this moment, a few dark figures might have been seen, but, unfortunately, were not, creeping cat-like in the direction of the unsuspecting Juan and the equally unconscious Murieta, Gonzalez, and the rest. It was well managed. By a sudden and concerted movement, the whole party were seized, overpowered, and securely bound before they were aware of what was going on. The Indians were in ecstasies at this almost unhoped-for success, for, had the least resistance been made, a single pistol cocked, or a knife drawn, they would have left the ground on the wings of the wind—so largely developed is the bump of caution[15] on the head of a California Indian! But cunning is equally developed, and serves their purposes quite as well sometimes as downright courage. As soon as this feat was accomplished, the woods became alive with forms, faces, and voices. A triumphal march was made with the captives to the capital.

They were stripped entirely naked, and their rich clothing covered the weather-beaten backs and scaly legs of
the Tejons; but great was the astonishment of the natives
when they discovered the sex of the three youthful cavaliers, who were kindly permitted, in pity for their mod-
esty, to wear some of the old cast-off shirts that lay
around in the dirt. The women were robbed of their jewelry to the amount of three thousand dollars and the men
of seven thousand dollars in gold dust, besides their riding animals and the stolen horses. They were left also
without a solitary weapon. Never were men so completely humiliated. The poor, miserable, cowardly Tejons
had achieved a greater triumph over them than all the
Americans put together! Joaquín looked grim for awhile,
but finally burst out into a loud laugh at his ridiculous
position, and ever afterwards endured his captivity with
a quiet smile. The most potent, grave, and reverend Señor
Sapatarra immediately dispatched one-half of the stolen
horses to the Oris Timbers, while he retained the other
according to agreement. He kept his prisoners of war in
custody for a week or two, debating in his mind whether
to make targets of them for his young men to practice ar-
chery upon, or to hang, burn, or drown them. He finally
sent word to "The Great Capitan," the county judge of
Los Angeles, that he had a party of Mexicans in custody
and wanted his advice on what to do with them. The
judge, supposing that the capture was the result of a little
feud between some "greasers"[16] and the Tejons, advised
him to release them. Accordingly, one fine morning, the
prisoners, under the supervision of Sapatarra surrounded
by his guard, who were armed with the revolvers and
knives which they had taken from the bandits, were led
forth from the village with such solemnity that they
imagined they were going to no other than a place of execution. Arrived at a group of live-oaks, they were

stripped entirely naked and bound each to a tree. Sapatarra made a long speech upon the merits of the important transaction which was about to occur, enlarging upon the enormity of the crime which had been committed (although it looked very much like self-condemnation in him to denounce stealing), and went off into extreme glorification over the magnanimity which would allow such great rascals to escape with their lives. He then gave orders to have them whipped. Seven large, stout fellows stepped out with a bunch of willow rods, each to his place, and gave the unfortunate party a very decent and thorough flogging. Sapatarra then declared the ends of justice satisfied and dismissed the prisoners from custody.

Poor fellows! They went forth into the wilderness as naked as on the day that they were born and stricken with a blanker poverty than the veriest beggar upon the streets of London, or New York, or any other proud city that raises its audacious head above its sea of crime and wretchedness into the pure light of Heaven. The biters were bit. The robbers were robbed, and loud and deep were the curses which Feliz, Juan, and Gonzalez pronounced upon Sapatarra and the whole Tejon Nation; but Joaquín rubbed his smarting back and laughed prodigiously—declaring upon his honor as a man that not a hair of old Sapatarra's head should be harmed. That night they slept without a stitch of covering; but, fortunately, it was near the summer, and the air possessed a merely pleasant coolness. The next day, in passing through an *arroyo*,[17] Reyes Feliz, who was behind, was attacked by a grizzly bear, and, being utterly defenceless, was horribly mangled. He begged his companions to leave him, as he must certainly die, and they could do him no good. After removing him to a shady place among some rocks and near to a stream of water, they left him to die—all but his sorrowing mistress, who resolved to remain with him whatever might befall. They turned to look as they departed, and the last they saw was the faithful girl with her lover's head upon her lap, pouring her tears upon him like a healing balm from her heart. Give me not a sneer, thou rigid righteous! for the love of woman is beautiful at all times, whether she smiles under gilded canopies in her satin garments or weeps over a world-hated criminal alone and naked in a desert.

After a day or two's travel, Joaquín and party arrived, nearly worn out, in the vicinity of the San Francisco Rancho at the head of the Tejon Pass where they met with Mountain Jim, one of their confederates, who had been out upon his "own hook" robbing and stealing for a few weeks then passed. He was astounded at the spectacle which they presented, and begged Joaquín to allow him the privilege of laughing one hearty laugh before he listened to any explanation of the mystery. The privilege was readily granted, and the jolly bandit went through the performance with great zest and unction, making the woods echo and re-echo with his most refreshing peals of merriment. The women hid themselves in the brush, and were like mother Eve when she sinned—conscious of their nakedness without being told of it.

The mystery being cleared up and explanation given in detail, Mountain Jim rode off to the rancho, or rather to his hiding-place in its vicinity, and soon returned with clothing for the party—shirts and pantaloons—but no dresses for females, at which, however, they did not grumble, preferring these garments, perhaps, to any other—at any rate, well satisfied to adopt any sort of dress which would relieve them of the very primitive style in which they then appeared. Mountain Jim also brought a couple of horses, one of which, a fine black animal, saddled and bridled in a most superb manner—he designed for his chief. He handed him, at the same time with presenting the horse, a Colt's six-shooter and a silver-mounted bowie-knife. Thus, in a few moments, was the naked and defenceless fugitive booted, spurred, and fully equipped—in an instant transformed into a powerful and dreaded outlaw; and this by the efficiency of that combination which his own daring genius had set on foot and successfully maintained. Having some mysterious power over persons then connected with the two wealthy ranchos, Camula and Santa Buenaventura—whether through a sentiment of fear with which he inspired them, or from a distinct understanding that they should harbor and assist him in consideration of a share of his plunders, I am not prepared to say—he sent Gonzalez and Juan with the women to visit those ranchos and obtain an outfit suitable for their business, with instructions for them to remain there until he should call or send for them. He and Mountain Jim rode back into the woods to the place at which he had left Reyes Feliz and his weeping companion. Contrary to all expectation, they found him not only alive but able to sit up. His faithful mistress had supplied him with the only food she could obtain, but which served much better than none—namely, a sweet-smelling root which grows in great abundance all over that region, resembling both in taste and appearance the common celery of our gardens; and also some red berries which grew on the bushes around her. She was nursing him tenderly and dressing his wounds with leaves—anxiously hoping that he would soon be well enough to proceed on their journey. Mountain Jim drew from his wallet some shirts and pantaloons, which he presented to the naked unfortunates—a most grateful sight and an opportunity to look decent of which they immediately availed themselves. With difficulty Reyes Feliz was mounted behind his brother-in-law, and Carmelita took her seat behind Mountain Jim, and off they rode in a gallop in the direction of the Mission of San Gabriel. Arriving in San Gabriel after night-fall, they went immediately to their usual meeting-place in an out-of-the-way house, and there very unexpectedly found Claudio and his band, who had returned from the State of Sonora sooner than expected, and, not finding his leader at Arroyo Cantoova, preferred going out on a marauding expedition to remaining idle. He had placed the horses with which he had been sent to Sonora upon a rancho well-known to Joaquín and where they would be perfectly safe till called for. In the vicinity of San Gabriel, he had committed many robberies since his return and had a purse amply filled with *the needful*, which he immediately tendered to his leader. But he had been greatly harrassed by Gen. Bean of that neighborhood, who had used every exertion to apprehend him and had compelled him several times, with his whole party, to seek safety in flight. The greater part of this news was highly gratifying to Joaquín, and he shook his faithful subordinate most cordially by the hand.

"But," said he, "we must never leave here, Claudio, till that man is killed. He is dangerous and we must put him out of the way."

Claudio assented with a grim nod of his head.

"I would like much now to see Three-Fingered Jack," said Joaquín, after a pause and a few moment's reflection. "Have you any idea where he is?"

"I don't know for a certainty," replied Claudio, "but there was a house burnt about ten miles from here the other night, and every soul murdered as they came out— men, women, and children—and I think *that* must positively be Three-Fingered Jack's work, and no other's."

Well provided with blankets, provisions, and a plenty of brandy, the bandits contented themselves to a stay of some two weeks at the Mission of San Gabriel. Reyes Feliz remained inactive, still attended by his faithful Carmelita. Horses were sent over to Camula and Santa Buenaventura after Joaquín's gentle love-mate and the wife of Gonzalez, who arrived in due time at the Mission, restored to their usually elegant appearance and glittering with jewelry. Gonzalez and Juan were at this time very carefully hiding from the lynx-eyes of a man whom they dreaded—namely, Capt. Harry Love, then deputy sheriff of Los Angeles County, who knew Gonzalez personally, and had caught a glimpse of that noted thief and his worthy colleague Juan on the skirts of the Buenaventura Rancho, which was known by a very few to be a harboring-place for Joaquín and closely watched on that account. In a day or two, news reached Joaquín that Gonzales had been arrested by Love while on a careless spree at a little "one-horse" grocery on a by-road that led up into the mountains and that Juan had made his escape after a very close clipping along the top of his head by a bullet from the Captain's revolver. He learned, in addition, that Love was hurrying off at the moment with his unfortunate confederate in the direction of the county seat of Los Angeles, where he would certainly be hung. Determined to rescue him at all hazards, he commanded Claudio to get his band in readiness, and, attended by Mountain Jim, he started at full speed to overtake Love and to save the life of his valuable subordinate. Having ridden all night and with the utmost urgency—as their bloody spurs and the foam of their horses attested—they came in sight of the object of their pursuit just at daybreak in the morning. Gonzalez, anticipating a rescue, looked back, and seeing them, waved his handkerchief. He was riding by the side of Love, unfettered, but totally in the power of his captor, being unarmed. This movement cost him his life; for Love, knowing the imminent risk which he ran in proceeding alone with a member of so formidable a

fraternity, no sooner saw the act than he drew his pistol
and drove a ball through the villain's heart. Casting a
glance behind him, he discovered a pursuing party, envel-
oped in a cloud of dust, coming like a whirlwind, and,
putting spurs to his horse, rode off at the top of his speed.
The bandits dashed up in a few moments to the place
where Gonzalez lay and found him a ghastly corpse. They
shed no tears but gnashed their teeth with rage and disappointment. It was of no use to follow Love, for his horse
was fresher than theirs, and he had already left them far
in the distance. Leaving the now worthless carcass of
their comrade, they rode over to the nearest rancho, and,
very coolly informing the owners that there was a dead
man lying on the side of the road, proceeded on their return to San Gabriel. Arrived at that place, Joaquín immediately learned two important facts—one of which was
that Three-Fingered Jack, with his party, was at the town
of Los Angeles, and the other that Capt. Wilson, deputy
sheriff of Santa Barbara County, had been at San Gabriel
making inquiries in relation to his whereabouts and most
diligently intent on capturing him, if possible. Wishing to
avoid Capt. Wilson and anxious to see Three-Fingered
Jack, he selected three of his best men out of Claudio's
band and started down to Los Angeles. He there met with
both Three-Fingered Jack and Valenzuela, who each gave
a good account of their operations, and were excessively
glad to see him. Joaquín, for curiosity, asked Garcia if he
had burnt a house down lately near San Gabriel, to which
he replied in the affirmative.

Remaining for a day or two at a regular hiding-place
which he had in that town and sallying out occasionally at
night to take his latitude, Joaquín ascertained that Capt.
Wilson was at one of the principal hotels making no con-
cealment of his purpose to take him, dead or alive. The
next night after this discovery, a great excitement was

raised in the street, and a crowd rushed up to see an apparently very hard fist-fight between two Indians in front of the hotel at which Wilson was stopping. He, in common with others, stepped out to witness it, and was looking on with much interest when a dashing young fellow rode up by his side on a fine horse, and stooping over his saddle-bow, hissed in his ear, "I am Joaquín." The astounded hearer started at the sentence, and had scarcely looked around before a pistol-ball penetrated his skull, and he fell dead to the earth. With his accustomed whoop, the daring murderer put spurs to his animal and galloped off. The fight between the Indians was a sham affair gotten up by Three-Fingered Jack to effect the very purpose which was consummated.

As the immediate consequence of this act, Los Angeles became too hot a place for the robbers to stay in; for the whole community was aroused and thirsting for vengeance. Accordingly Joaquín held a hasty conference with his followers which resulted in sending Valenzuela and band, accompanied by Mountain Jim, into San Diego County, with directions to steal horses and convey them to Arroyo Cantoova, while Three-Fingered Jack with his band should accompany his chief wherever he might choose to go. Choosing to return once more to San Gabriel, they started in that direction and met with no incident or individual on the road until they came to a dark hollow, walled on each side with precipitous rocks through which a noisy stream was leaping and glancing in the moonlight; at this place two helpless Chinamen were encamped by the foot of a sycamore tree, and, it being near eleven o'clock in the night, were sleeping off their fatigue and the effects of their luxurious pipes of opium. Their picks and prospecting pans showed them to be miners, who were most probably supplied with a due amount of cash, as Chinamen generally are. Joaquín was for riding

on, but Three-Fingered Jack could not resist the tempta-
tion of at least giving their pockets an examination. He,
therefore, dismounted and walked up to the unconscious
Celestials,[18] who were snoring very soundly in their blankets, and shook them. They awoke, and, seeing a horrible-
looking devil standing over and glaring upon them, raised
a hideous shriek, and, rising, fell upon their knees before
him with the most lugubrious supplications in a by no
means euphonious tongue. Jack told them to "dry up" but
they continued pleading for mercy when he knocked one
of them down with his revolver and, cocking it, presented
it at the head of the other, who closed his eyes in an agony
of despair. In a voice of thunder, he told the terrified
Chinamen to "shell out," or he would blow a hole through
him in a minute. Readily convinced of the truth of this remark, the poor fellow nervously jerked out his purse and
handed it to the robber, and, searching the pocket of his
companion, who lay stunned by his side, took out his also
and presented it with a shudder. The amount was small—
not more than twenty or thirty dollars—which so enraged
the sanguinary monster that he drew his knife and cut
both of their throats before Joaquín could possibly interfere to prevent it. The young chief, who always regretted
unnecessary cruelty but knew full well that he could not
dispense with so brave a man as Garcia, said nothing to
him but only groaned and rode on. The party reached San
Gabriel without further incident.

Gen. Bean, a man of influence and wealth, had, during
Joaquín's absence, been giving serious trouble to Claudio
and band, who had been compelled to lay out in the
woods to avoid him. Joaquín himself thought it prudent
to keep out of his way and lay concealed with Claudio for
the space of six weeks, having with him Three-Fingered
Jack and band. Portions of the banditti had regularly

watched every opportunity to kill Gen. Bean up to this time but had signally failed in every attempt. One evening, however, a spy having seen him start from his store at San Gabriel on horseback in the direction of his home a few miles off, Three-Fingered Jack and Joaquín started by themselves to head around him and way-lay the road. They had scarcely taken their positions behind some rocks before Bean rode up. Joaquín sprung out in front of him, and, seizing the bridle, which had a Spanish bit, jerked his horse back on his haunches, and, just at that moment, Three-Fingered Jack dragged him from the saddle and threw him upon the ground. At the moment that Jack laid hold of him, he was in the act of firing at Joaquín, but, being pulled back so suddenly, his pistol flew up many feet above the proper level, and was discharged into the empty air. Bean, being a powerful man, rose to his feet with Three-Fingered Jack upon him, and, drawing his knife, endeavored to use it, but his equally powerful antagonist seized his wrist with his left hand, and drawing in his turn a glittering bowie-knife, sheathed it three times in his breast, then, withdrawing the bloody blade, he rudely shoved him back, and the brave but unfortunate man fell dead at his feet. The ignoble wretch, not satisfied with the successful termination of the combat, displayed his brutal disposition by kicking the dead body in the face and discharging two loads from his revolver into the lifeless head.

Thus perished Gen. Bean, a generous, noble-hearted, and brave man. Had he been less brave, he might have exercised more caution and preserved his life; but he was a man who never knew fear.

After this outrage, which, though dark enough, was yet only an act of self-preservation on the part of Joaquín, he collected his whole party in the neighborhood of the

Mission and started again on his ever restless course. He
bent his way northward into Calaveras County, robbing
a few peddling Jews, two or three Frenchmen, and a
Chinaman, as he went along, and giving an American express agent a fearful race for his life on an open plain for
five or six miles, in which he distinctly heard no less than
twenty bullets whiz by his head, and arrived in the vicinity of the town of Jackson in the latter part of the month
of August.

Riding along one evening in advance of his men, as was
frequently his custom, he met an old acquaintance who
had been an esteemed friend in his more honest and
happy days, a young man whose name was Joe Lake.
Joaquín was delighted to see him, and rode up to his side
and embraced him, as they both sat on their horses, with
that generous warmth of feeling which made an otherwise unmeaning custom of the Mexicans, beautiful.

"Joe," said he, as he brushed a tear from his eyes, "I
am not the man that I was; I am a deep-dyed scoundrel,
but so help me God! I was driven to it by oppression and
wrong. I hate my enemies, who are almost all of the
Americans, but I love *you* for the sake of old times. I
don't ask you, Joe, to love or respect me, for an honest
man like you cannot, but I do ask you not to betray me. I
am unknown in this vicinity, and no one will suspect my
presence, if you do not tell that you have seen me. My
former good friend, I would rather do anything in the
world than kill you, but if you betray me, I will certainly
do it."

Lake assured him there was no danger, and the two
parted, for the wide gulf of dishonor yawned between
them, and they could never again be united. Lake rode
over to the little town of Ornetas, and, feeling it to be his
duty to warn the citizens that so dangerous a man was in
their midst, told a few Americans quite privately that he

had seen the bloody cut-throat Murieta. A Mexican was standing by, wrapped in his *serape*, who bent his head on his bosom and smiled. About sun-down of the next day, a solitary horseman, whose head was covered with a profusion of *red hair*, rode up very leisurely to the front of a trading-post, at which Lake and some other gentlemen were standing, politely raised his hat, and addressed an enquiry to Lake, which caused him to step forward from the crowd the better to converse.

"Is your name Lake?" said the red-haired stranger.

"The same," was the reply.

"Well, sir, I am Joaquín! you have *lied* to me."

Lake being unarmed, exclaimed, "Gentlemen, protect me," and sprung back towards the crowd. Several persons drew their revolvers, but not before the quick hand of Joaquín had presented his and pulled the trigger. The aim was fatal, and Lake fell in the agonies of death. The murderer wheeled his horse in an instant, and, by a sudden bound, passed the aim of the revolvers which were discharged at him. In another instant he was seen on the summit of a hill, surrounded by no less than fifty well-mounted men, with whom he slowly rode off. Such was the magical luck which pursued this man, following him like an invisible guardian fiend in every hour of his peril, and enabling him to successfully perform deeds which would turn any other man's blood cold. So perfect was the organization which he had established that that apparently harmless Mexican, who was standing near while Lake betrayed Joaquín, and who lived unsuspected in that very town, was none other than a paid member of his band who acted as a spy.

From this time until the middle of November, nothing definite is known of the movements of Joaquín, but rumors were rife of murders, robberies, and thefts, which are without much doubt attributable to him, and it is highly probable that the many horses which were stolen in this interval found their way to the Arroyo Cantoova, and from thence to Sonora. Indeed, as will be recollected, Valenzuela was expressly engaged in this business at that time, and in no other.

About the middle of November, Joaquín, with Claudio, Three-Fingered Jack, Reis—a member not mentioned before—Juan, who had managed after many narrow escapes to rejoin the band after the death of Gonzalez—and some fifty other followers were resting themselves and their horses at the Mission of San Luis Obispo in San Luis Obispo County. A portion of the band were also recruiting at Santa Margarita, not more than fifteen or twenty miles distant from the former place. There were persons connected at that time with both of these extensive ranchos who knew more about Joaquín's concerns than they cared to acknowledge. Their names are unknown to the writer at this time, but they can easily be ascertained should they insist upon appearing before the public.

While stopping at the first-named rancho, Joaquín one day took up *The Los Angeles Star*, a paper published at Los Angeles, and was reading the news when his sight seemed suddenly blasted, and he let the paper fall from his hands. His affrighted mistress sprang to his side, and clasping his hands, begged him to tell what was the matter. He shook his head for a moment, and the tears gushed from his eyes—aye, robber as he was—as he exclaimed, with quivering lips:

"Rosita, you will never see your brother again. Reyes Feliz is dead. He was hung two days ago by the people of Los Angeles."

Pierced with anguish, the fair girl sunk upon his bosom, and from her dark eyes, overshadowed by the rich, luxuriant hair, which fell around her like a midnight cloud—the storm of her grief poured itself forth in fast and burning drops, which fell like molten lead upon her lover's heart. Why should I describe it? It is well that woman should, like a weeping angel, sanctify our dark and suffering world with her tears. Let them flow. The blood which stains the fair face of our mother Earth may not be washed out with an ocean of tears.

To return to a simple narration of facts. It is indeed true that Reyes Feliz, in his seventeenth year, had met with what is almost always the outlaw's fate—an ignominious death upon the gallows. Having recovered from his wounds, he left San Gabriel and went down to Los Angeles, attended by his devoted Carmelita, where he had been only a few days before he was recognized by an American as one of a party who had once robbed him in the vicinity of Mokelumne Hill. Standing without the least suspicion of danger in a "fandango house" at Los Angeles, he was suddenly arrested and covered with irons; he was charged with being a party to the assassination of General Bean, and, although no evidence appeared to implicate him in this transaction, yet enough was elicited to show that he was undoubtedly a thief and a murderer. He was accordingly taken to the gallows, where he kissed the crucifix and made oath that he was innocent of the murder of General Bean but guilty in many other instances. Though doomed to die at so early an age—young, healthy, and full of the fine spirits which give a charm to early manhood—beloved as men are seldom loved, by the faithful girl who had left her pleasant home for him—a wild, untameable boy—he quailed not in the presence of death but faced it with a calm brow and tranquil smile. There came over him no shudder or paleness as the rope was adjusted around his neck, and he himself leaped from the platform just as it was about to fall from under him. Alas, for the unfortunate Carmelita! She wandered alone in the woods, weeping and tearing her hair, and many a startled ear caught the wail of her voice at midnight in the forest. She fled at the approach of a human footstep, but at last they found her cold and ghastly form stretched on a barren rock, in the still beauty of death. The Mexicans buried her by the side of her well-beloved Feliz, and the winds shall whisper as mournfully over their graves as if the purest and best of mortal dust reposed below. All-loving Nature is no respecter of persons,[19] and takes to her bosom all her children when they have ceased their wanderings, and eases their heartaches in her embracing arms. We may go down to our graves with the scorn of an indignant world upon us, which hurls us from its presence—but the eternal God allows no fragment of our souls, no atom of our dust, to be lost from his universe. Poised on our own immortality, we may defy the human race and all that exists beneath the throne of God!

A few days after the distressing news which they had heard, Joaquín and his sweet Rosita were sitting in front of an old building at the Mission, enjoying, as well as they could, the cool of the evening—for the month of November was still pleasant in the southern counties—when a Mexican rode up in a gallop and hastily dismounted. He advanced towards Joaquín, who rose at his approach, and, seeing that he was a stranger, gave him the secret sign by which any member of the organization might recognize another, though they had never met. It was satisfactorily returned, and the stranger immediately inquired for Joaquín and expressed a wish to see him. He was, of course, informed that he was addressing that individual himself, whereupon he proceeded to unfold the object of his mission.

"I am," said he, "most worthy Señor, deputed by a person whom you wot of, residing near the rancho of Gen. Pio Pico, to say to you that there is danger where you now are. A party of Americans, well armed and mounted, have passed the rancho Los Cayotes in this direction, and it is no doubt their intention to surprise you at your present retreat. I myself passed them this morning, without being perceived, encamped about fifteen miles from this place, and I seriously believe that you had better look out."

"Very well," replied the chief, without changing countenance, "this is as good as I want; hold yourself in readiness to serve me as a guide to their encampment, for I intend to surprise *them*."

Summoning Three-Fingered Jack and Claudio, he informed them of the facts which he had heard and of his intentions, directing them to prepare the band immediately for action. In an hour afterwards, the different members came galloping up from various parts of the rancho, booted, spurred, and equipped in brilliant style, to the number of forty-five men. They were fine-looking fellows, and scarcely any of them over thirty-five years of age. Under the guidance of the Los Cayotes messenger, who was furnished with a fresh horse, they started just as night set in upon their dangerous expedition. After a ride of two hours and a half, they arrived at their destination. The fires were still burning, but the camp was abandoned. It was too dark to follow a trail, and they stopped for the night. At daybreak they arose, mounted their horses, and pursued a very fresh trail which led through the woods, as if carefully to avoid the main roads. By the number of tracks, it was evident that they were in pursuit of a strong force. The trail led precisely in the course of San Luis Obispo, and it was apparent that the Americans had started for that place about the same time that Joaquín had left it; but he, having traveled the main road, thus missed them on the way. Arriving at ten o'clock within two miles of the Mission, he halted and sent a spy forward to examine and report, who returned in a short time with the information that the party, consisting of fifty men, had left the Mission at daylight on that morning with the evident purpose of taking the beaten road straight back to their encampment of the day before, the tracks of the banditti being still fresh on the ground. It was plain, therefore, that, finding unmistakable indications that the bandits had staid at their encampment and had followed their trail towards the Mission, they would hurry on to overtake them and would be able to make the entire circuit before sun-down of that day. The young chief clapped his hands together in perfect glee.

"We have them, boys! we have got them *dead*!" He wheeled his horse directly around and led his company about three miles back on the trail which they had just come, and halted at the junction of two deep gulches, rugged and shaggy with overhanging rocks. Directing his men to hide their horses at a distance of three or four hundred yards from the trail, he ordered them next to conceal themselves in the nooks and crevices of the surrounding bluffs. They lay there as still as death for about two hours, when the clatter of horses' feet was heard distinctly in the distance. Nearer and nearer they came, and, in a few minutes, a fine-looking young man with blue eyes and light hair rode up within twenty yards of Joaquín, followed by about fifty other Americans, armed with rifles and revolvers.

"I don't like the looks of this place at all," said the young man, and hardly had the words escaped his lips before the rocks blazed around him, and the sharp reports of twenty or thirty pistols rang in his ears. His hat was shot from his head, and his horse fell under him. A dozen of his followers bit the dust.

"Dismount, boys, and scale the rocks! Give them no

advantage! Face them in their very teeth! It is our only chance."

They sprang to the rocks at the word, each man to the quarter which he chose, and hand to hand bearded their hidden foes in their very dens. It could scarcely be called a battle between two distinct forces—it was rather a number of separate single combats, in which nothing could avail a man but his own right arm and dauntless heart. Joaquín sprung from his hiding-place to have a freer sweep of his arm, when he met at the very threshold the young Anglo-Saxon. A flash of recognition passed between them, and Joaquín turned as if to leap upon a rock at his right, but, at the moment that his antagonist jumped in that direction to intercept the movement, he wheeled to the left, and, throwing out his foot with a sudden and vigorous stroke, knocked the young man's heels from under him, and he fell with violence upon his face. Before he could rise, the wily bandit leaped upon him like a panther and sheathed his knife in his heart. It was too sad, but, as I have said before, an invisible guardian fiend pursued everywhere this extraordinary man. Having no time to repeat the blow, especially as it seemed unnecessary, he drew forth the dripping blade and rushed to another scene of the conflict. He was met at almost every step, and fought his way like a tiger, gashed and bleeding, but still strong and unfainting. Dead men lay upon every side, both Americans and Mexicans, and in front of Three-Fingered Jack were stretched five men with their skulls broken by the butt-end of his revolver, which he had used as a club after emptying its contents, and, at the moment that Joaquín's eye met him, he was stooping with glaring eyes and a hideous smile over a prostrate American, in whose long hair he had wound his left hand and across whose throat he was drawing the

coarse grained steel of his huge home-made bowie-knife.
With a shout of delight he severed the neckjoint and
threw the gaping head over the rocks. He was crazy with
the sight of blood and searched eagerly for another victim.
He scarcely knew his leader, and the latter had called to
him three times before he recovered his senses.

"Ah, Murieta," said he, smacking his lips together, "this
has been a great day. Damn 'em! how my knife lapped up
their blood."

The fight having now lasted for half an hour, and there
being no prospect that either party would conquer, so
equally were they matched, it gradually subsided, and
each side finally drew off from the other with a tacit understanding that they were mutually satisfied to cry quits.
Joaquín looked around and saw that he had lost twenty
men, among whom was the invaluable Claudio, and ascertained the loss on his enemies' side to be very nearly
the same, perhaps a little over. Mounting their horses,
the bandits rode off in silence toward San Luis Obispo
while the surviving Americans found as many of their
horses as had not left them during the conflict and retired
to their home in Santa Barbara County, having made ar-
rangements on the way for the burial of their deceased
comrades. During the following night, a company from
the Mission went over to the bloody scene with picks and
shovels and buried the dead bodies of the bandits near
the spot where they fell. On the next morning, Joaquín
summoned the Los Cayotes messenger and said to him:

"Go back and tell my friend, who sent you, that the danger is passed, and hand him this purse. For yourself, take
this one," handing him another well-filled buckskin bag.

Attention having been attracted to the San Luis Obispo
Rancho, the bandit thought it prudent to go elsewhere.
Accordingly, word was sent over to their friends who
were rusticating at Santa Margarita to join them, and

they forthwith started to a well-known harboring place not more than a *thousand miles* from José Ramune Carrejo's Rancho. Here they remained until such as were wounded recovered their usual health and strength—and here, again, Joaquín heard news similar to that which shocked him at San Luis Obispo, viz., that Mountain Jim had been hung in San Diego. This misfortune happened to the jolly robber from his own carelessness. He and Valenzuela had stopped at a drinking-shop on the San Diego River, some fifteen or twenty miles from the bay of that name, and had taken a glass of execrable brandy when a party of four or five Americans rode up and alighted, who looked so very suspiciously at Valenzuela and partner, that the former took his friend out and told him that it was his opinion they both had better leave as quick as possible. Mountain Jim was under the influence of liquor, and, laughing at what he chose to term the silly fears of Valenzuela, he went back into the house swearing and swaggering. Pretty soon after, a dozen more Americans approached on horseback, seeing whom Valenzuela mounted into his saddle and called to Jim to come along. But Jim only laughed and took another glass of liquor.

"Curse the fool!" muttered the bandit, "he will be the death of both of us. For my part, I will keep my own distance from those scurvy-looking fellows, at any rate."

The new party no sooner arrived than they rushed up to the door of the drinking-house and drew their revolvers—a scuffle ensued inside, and Valenzuela, well aware of what was going on and that it was useless to contend against such great odds, merely fired one shot into the crowd at the door, which took effect in the abdomen of one of the party, and, wheeling his horse, broke off like a thunderbolt. Several of the Americans pursued him, but his fine, swift animal distanced them so far that they might as well have attempted to catch the red-winged spirit of a storm. Poor Mountain Jim! He was never destined to tread the mountains again. He was taken to the town of San Diego, and hung with as little ceremony as if he had been a dog. Well fitted was he to grace a gallows, for his merits certainly entitled him to a distinguished elevation.

From his present stopping place, Joaquín sent a messenger about the first of December to the Arroyo Cantoova to see Valenzuela if he was there, and, if he was absent to await his return in order to inform him that it was made his duty to continue the business in which he was engaged through the entire winter, or until such time as Joaquín should arrive at the rendezvous. The messenger returned after a few days and stated that he had found Valenzuela and band at the Arroyo with tents pitched and a herd of fine horses, amounting to between five and six hundred, feeding on the pasture; and that the bold leader had signified a willing obedience to his chief's mandate.

"He is a glorious fellow," exclaimed Joaquín. "He didn't practice under that hardened old priest, Jurata, without learning something."

Spies were now ranging the country every day, picking up valuable information—and, among other things, it was ascertained that an opinion prevailed that Joaquín had gone to the State of Sonora. Thinking it a favorable time, he issued forth with his entire force, uniting Three-Fingered Jack's party with Claudio's which last was now under the leadership of Reis—and started up into Mariposa County for the purpose of plunder.

On the road that leads from Dead Man's Creek to the Merced River, he met four Frenchmen, six Germans, and three Americans, walking and driving mules before them, packed with provisions, blankets, and mining utensils. Having so large a party with him, numbering about thirty men, he had no difficulty in stopping the travelers as long as he wished to detain them. His men stood around with pistols cocked while Joaquín dismounted, and, walking up to a terrified Frenchman who was armed with a revolver which he was afraid to use, took him by the top of the head, and jerking him around once or twice, slapped him across the face with his open hand, and told him to "shell out." The Frenchman hauled out a well-filled purse, and was handing it over when others of his companions made a show to draw their pistols and defend their gold-dust. The robbers were too quick for them, and more than half of the unfortunate miners were shot down in their tracks. Joaquín brandished his glittering blade in the faces of the survivors and threatened to cut every one of their windpipes if they didn't hand out "what little loose change" they had about them, in half a minute! His polite request was complied with, and the little loose change amounted to about $15,000. He then bestowed a kick or two on some of the number as a parting tribute of regard and told them to "roll on." Three-Fingered Jack insisted on killing the whole company, but the chief overruled him.

Riding forward after this transaction, they had not gone more than two miles when they met a Chinaman with a long tail,[20] carrying a large bundle suspended at each end of a stick laid across his shoulders, walking leisurely along with his head bent to the ground. Looking up and seeing so large a number of armed men before him, his eyes rolled in sudden fear, and he ducked his half-shaved head in unmistakable homage and respect to—the revolvers and bowie-knives which met his vision. No one harmed him, and he shuffled on vastly gratified and relieved. He had passed only a few minutes when he was heard howling and screaming in the most harrowing manner; and, looking back, they discovered the horrified Celestial with his tail flying in the wind, running towards them at the top of his speed, with arms wildly sawing the air, and bundle-*less*, while the ground clattered under his wooden shoes; and just behind him, with blazing eyes, and his huge home-made knife in his right hand, appeared Three-Fingered Jack, who had stopped at a spring and was tying his horse to a bush at the moment that the Chinaman came up. It was too good an opportunity to be lost, and he darted like a wild hyena at the astounded Oriental, who applied himself to his heels with the utmost vigor that he could command. Joaquín bowed himself upon the saddle in a convulsion of laughter at the ridiculous appearance of the Chinaman but speedily confronted Jack and told him to stop. Woh Le fell upon his knees in deepest adoration of his preserver. Joaquín bade him go on his way and, laughingly, reprimanded Jack for wanting to kill so pitiful a looking creature.

"Well," said Jack, "I can't help it; but, somehow or other, I love to smell the blood of a Chinaman. Besides, it's such easy work to kill them. It's a kind of luxury to cut their throats."

Proceeding across the woods and mountains, the banditti in a few days struck the main road leading from the town of Mariposa to Stockton, in San Joaquin County. Robbing once in a while as they went along, they arrived late one night at a ferry on the Tuolumne River in Tuolumne County, and finding the boat locked to the shore so that they could not exercise the privilege of crossing themselves, which was their usual custom, they rode up to the ferryman's house and very nearly beat the door down before they could arouse him. He came out at last with a terrified look and asked what they wanted.

"We want to cross the river," replied Joaquín; "and before doing so we wish to obtain from you the loan of what spare cash you may have about you. We have the best evidence of the urgency of our request," cocking his pistol and presenting it close to the fellow's head.

"Never mind the evidence, Señor; I believe you without it. I will certainly loan you all I have got."

So saying, he lit a candle and got out a purse from under his pillow, containing a hundred dollars.

"Come," said Jack, bursting a cap at his head, "you have got more"; and was cocking his pistol for another trial when Joaquín very fiercely told him to know his place. Turning to the trembling ferryman, he said,

"Is this all you have got?"

"Precisely all, Señor; but you are welcome to it."

"I won't take it," said the young chief with a flush of pride; "you are a poor man and you never injured me. Put us over the river and I will pay you for your trouble."

I mention this incident merely to show that Murieta in his worst days had yet a remnant of the noble spirit which had been his original nature and to correct those who have said that he was lost to every generous sentiment.

The party arrived in the neighborhood of Stockton without further incident, after two day's travel, and camped on the plain under an oak grove, about three miles from that place. They were seen at their encampment but not suspected. Indeed, it was then, as it is now, so common a thing to see companies of men engaged in the various occupations of packers, cattle-drovers, horse-traders, hunters, etc., stationed by the banks of some cool stream, or resting under the shade of trees at a distance from any house, or with their tents pitched in some lonely place for weeks at a time—that it was scarcely just to suspect a party to be criminal, merely from circumstances like these. The knowledge of everybody that it was the habit among all classes to go armed and to camp out in every sort of a place materially aided the banditti in their movements, for it gave them the opportunity to remain perfectly safe until they chose to avow their real characters by some open outrage and villainy.

One fine Sunday morning, while the bells were ringing
for church in the goodly city of Stockton, and well-dressed
gentlemen were standing at the corners of the streets,
marking with critical eyes the glancing feet and the flaunt-
ing dresses of the ladies who swept by them in the halo of
beauty and perfumery, a fine-looking man whom they
had never seen before—having long, black hair hanging
over his shoulders and a piercing black eye—rode through
the streets, carelessly looking at the different objects
which happened to attract his attention. So finely was he
dressed, and so superbly was his horse caparisoned that,
without seeming to know it, he was observed of all ob-
servers.

"What a splendid looking fellow!" said the ladies.

"He must be a young Mexican Grandee[21] at the least, on
a journey of pleasure," said one.

"I think," said another, "it must be General Vallejo's[22]
son."

"I don't believe he has any," said a third; and they became so much interested in their conjectures about the
young man that it is very doubtful if they paid much attention to the very prosy minister who was then acting as
the "bright and shining light" amidst the surrounding
darkness.

The youthful cavalier, after attracting uncommon attention by riding over the city, finally stopped at the side
of a house, upon which were posted several notices—one
reading as follows:

"FOR SAIL.

the surscribur ophfers for sail a yaul-bote hicht at the hed of
the Slew terms cash or kabbige turnips and sich like will bea
tayken."

To which fine specimen of polite literature was appended the name of a worthy citizen, who was then fishing for his living, but has since been fishing for various offices in the county.

Another one was a "notis" that some person either wanted to hire some one else or be hired himself as a cook—it was impossible to tell which.

A third was an auctioneer's notice:

"Honor before the 25 da of Dec I will offur to the hiest bider a brown mule ate yeer old, a gilding 16 hans hi, and a span of jacks consistin of long years and a good voyce."

I have a notion to publish the name signed to this rare advertisement, especially as the auctioneer seems to have been something of a wag as well as ignoramus. But, perhaps, it will be better not. A fourth was headed, in good English and a fair running hand:

"Five Thousand Dollars Reward for Joaquín, dead or alive,"

and stated that the citizens of San Joaquin County offered that amount for the apprehension or the killing of that noted robber.

Seeing this, the young Mexican dismounted, and taking out his pencil, wrote something underneath, and leisurely rode out of town. No less than a dozen persons, stimulated by curiosity, went to the paper to see what was written, when they read the following in pencil:

"I will give $10,000.   JOAQUÍN."

Numerous were the exclamations of astonishment at this discovery, and nothing else was talked of for a week, among the ladies at least, who got hold of the fact almost before it was discovered and insisted each to the other that they had remarked that the young man had a peculiarly wild and terrible look, and they had suspected very strongly, though they had never mentioned it to any one, that it was none other than the noted personage whom it proved to be.

Joaquín appeared on this occasion in his real features. He frequently went afterwards, however, into that city completely disguised and learned many things important for him to hear. Ascertaining one evening that a schooner would go down the slough in a few hours, bound for San Francisco, on board of which were two miners from San Andreas in Calaveras County with heavy bags of gold dust who designed to take their departure for the States, he took three of his men who were lounging around town with him and, jumping into a skiff, shot down the slough, and tying up his boat in a bend of the water, hid in the *tules*[23] and patiently waited for the schooner to come along. The mosquitoes bit him unmercifully, and he was almost tempted to abandon the enterprise on their account, but the prospect of so good a haul was, on reflection, not to be resisted. He cursed himself for not bringing some matches with which he might have kindled a fire and sought the protection of its smoke; but perseverance is always rewarded if the object desired lies in the bounds of possibility, and, waiting like a martyr for three mortal hours in those *tules*, which are a perfect "mosquito kingdom" where huge gallinippers reign as the aristocracy, he at last saw the white-sheeted schooner stealing along in the crooks and turns of *just the crookedest stream in the whole world*, so narrow and so completely hid in its windings by the tall flags which overspread the plains for many miles to the right and left, that the white sail looked like a ghost gliding along over the waving grass. As the vessel came opposite, Joaquín and companions shoved their boat out into the stream, and tying it to the schooner's side, leaped on board of her and commenced firing without saying a word. They shot down the two young men who managed the vessel before they had time to use their double-barreled shot-guns, which they always carried for the purpose of shooting water-fowl in the slough and up the San Joaquin River, and, rushing aft, attacked the two miners, who had risen at the report of the pistols, and were standing with their revolvers drawn and cocked, ready for action. They and the robbers fired simultaneously. Two of Joaquín's men fell dead on the deck, and the miners fell at the same time. Their wallets were soon stripped from them by Joaquín and his surviving companion, and, finding some matches, they set fire to the vessel and left her to burn down. They rowed their skiff to the head of the slough in Stockton and wended their way back to their encampment. Ere daylight, there was no trace of murder on the slough, but a dark hulk which was barely visible on the water's edge. By this operation Joaquín realized $20,000. Having now between forty and fifty thousand dollars in gold dust, he ordered his bands to pack up and started for the rendezvous of Arroyo Cantoova, passing by José Ramune Carrejo's Rancho and taking the lovely Rosita along with him, who had been staying there during his trip to Stockton.

He reached the Arroyo about the middle of the day, and it was a beautiful sight that met his eye, as he gazed over the extensive valley and saw a thousand fine horses feeding on the rich grass or galloping with flowing manes and expanded nostrils in graceful circles over the plain.

"Valenzuela has done his work well," said the elated chief, "ten times better than I had expected he would."

Seeing one of his herdsmen looking at him a short distance off as if endeavoring to recognize him, he rode up to him and asked him in reference to Valenzuela.

"He has been gone," said the vaquero, "about a week—we look for him every day."

The newly arrived party then rode up to the tents under the trees and dismounted. The busy cooks hurried up the fires, and the fresh venison and bear meat was soon smoking on the irons and emiting a most delicious savor, such as tempts the appetite of a hardy pioneer. Broiled quails and grouse, sweet and oily, the latter of which had been brought from the tall spruce trees at a hight of three hundred feet by the long, maple-stocked, and silver-mounted rifles which stood at the corner of one of the tents, were hanging in front of the blaze, suspended by their necks to branching sticks driven into the ground. The hot coffee steamed up from the large pot with a most stimulating effect; everything was spread forth in super-abundance, scattered over a large white cloth that covered a few yards square of green grass, and at a signal from the cooks, who were also the waiters, forty fierce and hungry brigands sat down and, with the utmost expedition consistent with respect for their leader, made havoc among the victuals. Just at this moment, a mounted company dashed up at full speed, giving the well-known whoop by which they could be recognized as friends, and dismounted. It was Valenzuela and a portion of his band, the remainder of whom soon after came in, driving two hundred and fifty thoroughbred American horses before them. The circle was enlarged, the cooks went to work afresh, and soon the whole banditti, who were all united for the first time after many months, were seated at the ample banquet. Generous wines stood sparkling in their midst with which scarcely any refused to refresh themselves. Conversation flowed freely, and each one had a tale to tell of hair-breadth escapes and daring deeds. After hearing a brisk series of bloody narrations, Joaquín turned to Valenzuela and said:

"My brave brother, you have never been very communicative in regard to your former life; let us hear an incident or two that happened to you when you served under the daring Padre Jurata. By the Holy Virgin! you must have had some awful experiences in those days."

Valenzuela related the following story:

"One night when the robber-priest and myself, who was his Lieutenant, and a dozen others were encamped by a small lake up in the mountains near to Cerro Gordo, which had recently been the battle-ground of the American and Mexican forces, some American horses which had escaped riderless from the scene of slaughter had wandered into the hills and fallen into our hands, and we expected that a party of Yankees would certainly get on their track and follow them up. We wanted Jurata to put out the fires, but he said no, he wanted the Americans to come on, and if the light was extinguished they would not be able to find him. He ordered more fuel to be put on, and the highly combustible pine-knots sent up a blaze that lit the woods for miles around. We had sat up about two hours after supper when he heard the approach of horsemen, the steel-shod hoofs ringing clearly against the rocky trail which led to our encampment. A moment after, perfect silence reigned, and we looked and listened in vain for the approaching party. Jurata suddenly sprung up after a few moments and exclaimed:

"'They are so still they must be slily creeping on to us, the damned cougars! let us get behind the trees.'

"We were just in the act of obeying this suggestion when a dozen shots rung from the adjacent shadows which bordered our fire, and no less than thirty gigantic Yankees rushed into our circle. Six of our men had fallen at the crack of their guns, and there were only eight of our number left to contend against the terrible odds opposed to us. Jurata cried out:

"'Let us lead them out of the light of the fires!'

"We sought shelter instantaneously in the rocks and stood at bay. On they came with their revolvers cocked and shivered the rocks around us with their bullets. We returned the fire with our own six-shooters, which, thanks to the American smugglers along the coast, we were amply supplied with, and heard many an ominous groan at each report. But they were so much superior to us in number that they shot at least four times to our once, and I saw that we must inevitably be overpowered. Five of my companions, who survived the shots at the fire, lay around me mortally wounded, and there were only Jurata, and myself, and one other left. We rushed from our temporary shelter, in which we would soon have been completely hemmed and at the mercy of our enemies, and, swinging down a precipice thirty feet high by some oak branches which over-hung it, hid ourselves noiselessly at the base. To and fro above our heads we distinctly heard the hurrying foot-steps of our pursuers. Finally one of them exclaimed:

"'These branches here are twisted and broken as if they had let themselves down this bluff.'

"Whereupon a dozen long-legged, brawny fellows came dangling over us. They had scarcely struck the ground before three of them bit the dust, and another instant had not elapsed before another discharge of our revolvers brought down two more, at which crisis others of the attacking party had come around below the bluffs, and before we had time to take breath, commenced firing. The splinters of the rocks and the bark of the trees flew around us as if we had been made the mark of congregated lightnings, and we were fain to get away from there. We set our teeth together and passed within ten feet of their guns, bounding like wild bucks. We made our escape, severely wounded, however, and dragged our aching limbs over the mountains to our rendezvous, where we found protection and medicine for our wounds in the midst of our brother guerrillas who had remained at home. I know of no fight in my whole experience so severe and soul-harrowing as that one."

"A good deal like one which we had," replied Joaquín, "a few miles from San Luis Obispo, when you, Valenzuela, were absent below, in which we lost the twenty brave men whom you miss from this circle. Three-Fingered Jack did the hardest fighting then that I ever saw. He was perfectly delirious and so blind with excitement that he was about to attack me for an enemy."

The afternoon and evening were consumed in reminiscences like these.

On the following morning, Joaquín collected his bands around him, numbering, from a late accession of new "fighting members" as he called them, one hundred men, and explained to them fully his views and purposes.

"I am at the head of an organization," said he, "of two thousand men whose ramifications are in Sonora, Lower California, and in this State. I have money in abundance deposited in a safe place. I intend to arm and equip fifteen hundred or two thousand men and make a clean sweep of the southern counties. I intend to kill the Americans by 'wholesale,' burn their ranchos, and run off their property at one single swoop so rapidly that they will not have time to collect an opposing force before I will have finished the work and found safety in the mountains of Sonora. When I do this, I shall wind up my career. My brothers, we will then be revenged for our wrongs, and some little, too, for the wrongs of our poor, bleeding country. We will divide our substance and spend the rest of our days in peace. I am now preparing for this grand climax, and this is the reason, Valenzuela, that I have kept you so busy collecting horses."

The banditti shouted in loud applause of their gallant leader. Their eyes kindled with enthusiasm at the magnificent prospect which he presented to them, and they could scarcely contain themselves in view of the astounding revelations which he had made. They had entertained no adequate idea of the splendid genius which belonged to their chief, although they had loved and admired him throughout his dangerous career. They were fired with new energy, and more than ever willing and anxious to obey him at all hazards and under the most disadvantageous circumstances.

On this same day he dispatched a remittance of $50,000 to his secret partner in Sonora under a strong force commanded by Valenzuela and directed Three-Fingered Jack, with fifty men, to drive off to the same State a thousand head of the horses which had been collected. Joaquín was accordingly left at the rendezvous with twenty-five men, who had nothing to do but kill game, and attend to their horses, and clean their arms. The wife of Gonzalez was there, who had consoled her widowhood by accepting a huge fellow as her husband by the name of Guerra, who looked like a grizzly bear more than a human being. He was not so kind to her as Gonzalez had been, and, one night while he was asleep, she was about to cut his throat when Joaquín, who was lying in the same tent, fiercely told her to behave herself and assured her with an emphasis that he would hold her responsible if Guerra was ever found dead about camp. She threw her knife spitefully towards Joaquín and laid down again by her adorable spouse, who snored in blissful ignorance of his wife's affectionate purpose.

Lounging in his tent one misty day—for the rainy

season had set in—Joaquín was aroused from the luxurious lap of his mistress by one of his sentinels, who galloped up and informed him that he had just discovered a fresh trail through the grass, about a mile and a half below on the Cantoova Creek, and, from appearances, he should judge there were eight or ten men. It was important to keep a sharp lookout and to allow no Americans to leave that valley with the knowledge that it was occupied by any body of men whatever, as such a circumstance would materially interfere with the gigantic plans projected. Accordingly, it was not long before Joaquín was mounted upon one of his swiftest horses and accompanied by fifteen picked men. They proceeded to the trail indicated by the sentinel and rode rapidly for two hours, which brought them in sight of ten Americans, who halted in curious surprise and waited for them to come up.

"Who are you?" said Joaquín, "and what is your business in these parts?"

They replied that they were hunters in search of bears and deer.

"We are hunters, also," rejoined the bandit, "and are camped just across the plain here. Come over with us, and let us have a chat. Besides, we have some first-rate liquor at our camp."

Suspecting nothing wrong, the hunters accompanied them, and, having dismounted at the tents and turned out their horses to graze, found themselves suddenly in a very doubtful position. They were surrounded by a company more than double their own who made demonstrations not at all grateful to their sight, and in a few moments they realized the bitter fact that they were driven to the extremity of a hopeless struggle for their lives. They remonstrated with Joaquín against so shameless an act as the cold-blooded murder of men who had never injured him.

"You have found me here," he replied, "and I have no guarantee that you will not betray me. If I do not tell you who I am, you will think it no harm to say that you have seen a man of my description; and, if I do tell you, then you will be certain to mention it at the first opportunity."

At this moment a young man, originally from the wilds of Arkansas, not more than eighteen years of age, advanced in front of his trembling comrades and, standing face to face with the robber-chief, addressed him in a firm voice to the following effect:

"I suspect strongly who you are, sir. I am satisfied that you are Joaquín Murieta. I am also satisfied that you are a brave man, who would not unnecessarily commit murder. You would not wish to take our lives, unless your own safety demanded it. I do not blame you, following the business you do, for desiring to put an effectual seal of silence on our tongues. But listen to me just a moment. You see that I am no coward. I do not look at you with the aspect of a man who would tell a falsehood to save his life. I promise you faithfully for myself, and in behalf of my companions, that if you spare our lives, which are completely in your power, not a word shall be breathed of your whereabouts. I will myself kill the first man who says a word in regard to it. Under different circumstances, I should take a different course, but *now*, I am conscious that to spare our lives will be an act of magnanimity on your part, and I stake my honor, not as an American citizen, but as a man, who is simply bound by justice to himself, under circumstances in which no other considerations can prevail, that you shall not be betrayed. If you say you will spare us, we thank you. If you say no, we can only fight till we die, and you must lose some of your lives in the conflict."

Joaquín drew his hand across his brow, and looked thoughtful and undecided. A beautiful female approached him from the tent near by and touched him on the shoulder.

"Spare them, Joaquín," she tremulously whispered, and, looking at him with pleading eyes, retired softly to her seat again.

Raising his fine head with a lofty look, he bent his large clear eyes upon the young American, as if he would read him like an outspread page. He answered his glance with a look so royally sincere that Joaquín exclaimed with sudden energy:

"I will spare you. Your countrymen have injured me, they have made me what I am, but I scorn to take the advantage of so brave a man. I will risk a look and a voice like yours, if it should lead to perdition. Saddle their horses for them," he said to his followers, "and let them depart in peace."

The party were very soon mounted again, and, showering blessings on Joaquín, who had become suddenly transformed into an angel in their estimation, they took their leave. I have never learned that the young man, or any of his party, broke their singular compact, and, indeed, it seems to me that it would have been very questionable morality in them to have done so, for certainly, however much they owed to society, it would have been a suicidal act to refuse to enter into such an agreement, and, as nothing but a firm conviction that they intended to keep their word could have induced Joaquín to run so great a risk, they were bound to preserve their faith inviolate. If they had a right to purchase their lives at the price of silence, they had an equal right, and not only that, but were morally bound, to stand up to their bargain. It would be well if men were never forced into such a position, but society has no right, after it has happened, to wring from them a secret which belongs to *them* and not to the world. In such matters God is the only judge.

The month of December was drawing to a close, and the busy brain of the accomplished chief had mapped out the full plan of his operations for the new year just at hand. It was the year which would close his short and tragical career with a crowning glory—a deed of daring and of power which would redeem with its refulgent light the darkness of his previous history and show him to aftertimes, not as a mere outlaw, committing petty depredations and robberies, but as a *hero* who has revenged his country's wrongs and washed out her disgrace in the blood of her enemies.

It was time for Three-Fingered Jack and Valenzuela to return from Sonora, and Joaquín waited patiently for their arrival in order to replenish his purse largely during the first months of the new year so that he might execute his magnificent purpose without embarrassment or obstruction. In a few days, Garcia and Valenzuela returned, accompanied by an old guerrilla comrade of the latter, named Luis Vulvia. The two had lost five men from their bands, killed in several skirmishes on their way back, with the citizens of Los Angeles County. Further than this, they had received no injury, and were in fine health and spirits, although their horses were somewhat jaded. Each leader handed to Joaquín a well-filled purse of gold coin. Having rested two days, the major portion of the banditti mounted fresh horses, and leaving the remainder, numbering twenty-five men, at the rendezvous under the command of Guerra, with whom they also left the females, not thinking it prudent, in view of the bloody scenes which would be enacted, to take them along, they set out for Calaveras County.

They had not been gone more than three days before a quarrel arose between Guerra and his affectionate wife, which ended in his giving her a wholesome thrashing. She submitted to the infliction with great apparent humility, but the next morning at breakfast time when Guerra was called and did not come, several of his companions went into his tent to arouse him and found him stone-dead. There was no sign of violence on his body, and it remained a complete mystery how he died. He had been a hard drinker, and, finally, his death was attributed to an over-indulgence the night before. But the fact of the case was, that unconscious sleeper had received at midnight just one drop of hot lead into his ear, tipped from a ladle by a small and skillful hand. Byron[24] has said in one of his misanthropic verses:

> "Woman's tears, produced at will,
> Deceive in life, unman in death."[25]

and the truth of this bitter asseveration was partially illustrated when the inconsolable widow wept so long and well over the husband whom she, like a second, nay, the thousandth jezebel, had made a corpse. It is barely possible, however, that her tears were those of remorse. She accepted for her third husband a young fellow in the band at the rendezvous named Isidora Conejo, who loved her much more tenderly than did the brutal Guerra, whom she so skillfully put out of the way. This young man was a few years her junior, but she looked as youthful as himself. Twice widowed, her sorrows had not dimmed the lustre of her eyes, or taken the gloss from her rich dark hair, or the rose from her cheeks. Her step was as buoyant as ever, the play of her limbs as graceful, the heave of her impulsive bosom as entrancing, and her voice as full of music as if she had never lost Gonzalez or murdered Guerra. There are some women who seem never to grow old. As each successive spring renews the plumage of the birds, so with them the passing years add fresh beauty to their forms, and decay long lingers ere he has the heart to touch their transcendent loveliness with his cold and withering fingers. The fascinating Margarita was one of these.

Joaquín with his party, fully bent on the most extensive mischief, entered Calaveras County about the middle of December. This county was then, as it is now, one of the richest in the State of California. Its mountains were veined with gold—the beds of its clear and far-rushing streams concealed the yellow grains in abundance—and the large quartz-leads, like the golden tree of the Hesperides,[26] spread their fruitful branches abroad through the hills. Its fertile valleys bloomed with voluptuous flowers over which you might walk as on a carpet woven of rainbows—or waved with the green and mellow harvests, whose ready music charmed the ear. The busy wheels of the sawmills with their glittering teeth rived the mighty pines, which stood like green and spiral towers, one above another, from base to summit of the majestic peaks. Long tunnels, dimly lighted with swinging lamps or flickering candles, searched far into the bowels of the earth for her hidden secrets. Those which were abandoned served as dens for the cougar and wolf, or, more frequently, the dens of thieves.

Over this attractive field for his enterprizes, Joaquín scattered his party in different directions. He entrusted Reis with the command of twenty men, Luis Vulvia with that of twenty-five, retaining about fifteen for his own use among whom was the terrible Three-Fingered Jack and the no less valuable Valenzuela, and employed the remainder as spies and bearers of news from one point of action to another. Reis went up to the head waters of the Stanislaus River between whose forks the rich valleys, covered with horses, afforded a fine theater for his operations. On all the mountain-fed branches and springs of these forks, the picks and shovels of a thousand miners were busy, and the industrious Chinese had pitched their little, cloth villages in a hundred spots, and each day hurried to and fro like innumerable ants, picking up the small but precious grains. Luis Vulvia—as daring a man as Claudio and as cunning— proceeded to the head waters of the Mokelumne River; and detached portions of these two bands, at intervals, ranged the intermediate space. Joaquín himself had no particular sphere but chose his ground according to circumstances. Keeping Three-Fingered Jack with him most of the time, he yet, once in a while, gave him the charge of a small party with liberty to do as he pleased—a favor which the bloody monster made good use of; so much so that scarcely a man whom he ever met, rich or poor, escaped with his life. The horse which this hideous fellow rode might have rivaled *Bucephalus*[27] in breadth of chest, high spirit, and strength of limb, united with swiftness. No one but a powerful man could have rode him; but Three-Fingered Jack, with a fine Mexican saddle (the best saddles in the world) fastened securely with a broad girth made of horse hair as strong as a band of iron, and curbing him with a huge Spanish bit—with which he might have rent his jaw— managed the royal animal with ease. To see this man, with his large and rugged frame in which the strength of a dozen common men slumbered—his face and forehead scarred with bullets and grooved with the wrinkles of grim thoughts, and his intensely lighted eyes glaring maliciously, like caverned demons, under his shaggy brows— to see such a man mounted upon a raven-black horse whose nostrils drew the air like a gust of wind into his broad chest, whose wrathful hoof pawed the ground as if the spirit of his rider inspired him, and whose wild orbs rolled from side to side in untameable fire—would aptly remind one of old Satan himself, mounted upon a hell- born beast, after he had been "let loose for a thousand years."[28]

Among the many thrilling instances of the daring and

recklessness of spirit which belonged to Joaquín, there is one which I do not feel at liberty to omit—especially as it comes naturally and properly in this connection. Shortly after he parted from Reis and Luis Vulvia, he went up into the extreme north of the county. There, at the head of a branch of the South Fork of the Mokelumne River, in a wild and desolate region near the boundary line of Calaveras and El Dorado Counties, were located a company of miners, consisting of twenty-five men. They were at a long distance from any neighbors, having gone there well armed on a prospecting tour which resulted in their finding diggings so rich that they were persuaded to pitch their tents and remain. One morning while they were eating their breakfast on a flat rock—a natural table which stood in front of their tents—armed as usual with their revolvers, a young fellow with very dark hair and eyes rode up and saluted them. He spoke very good English and they could scarcely make out whether he was a Mexican or an American. They requested him to get down and eat with them, but he politely declined. He sat with one leg crossed over his horse's neck very much at his ease, conversing very freely on various subjects, until Jim Boyce, one of the partners who had been to the spring after water, appeared in sight. At the first glance on him, the young horseman flung his reclining leg back over the saddle and spurred his horse. Boyce roared out:

"Boys, that fellow is *Joaquín*; d—n it, shoot him!" At the same instant, he himself fired but without effect.

Joaquín dashed down to the creek below with headlong speed and crossed with the intention, no doubt, to escape over the hills which ran parallel with the stream, but his way was blocked up by perpendicular rocks, and his only practicable path was a narrow digger-trail[29] which led along the side of a huge mountain, directly over a ledge of rocks a hundred yards in length, which hung beatling over

Captain Harry Love

the rushing stream beneath in a direct line with the hill upon which the miners had pitched their tents, and not more than forty yards distant. It was a fearful gauntlet for any man to run. Not only was there danger of falling a hundred feet from the rocks, but he must run in a parallel line with his enemies, and in pistol-range, for a hundred yards. In fair view of him stood the whole company with their revolvers drawn. He dashed along that fearful trail as if he had been mounted upon a spirit-steed, shouting as he passed:

"I am Joaquín! kill me if you can!"

Shot after shot came clanging around his head, and bullet after bullet flattened on the wall of slate at his right. In the midst of the first firing, his hat was knocked from his head, and left his long black hair streaming behind him. He had no time to use his own pistol, but, knowing that his only chance lay in the swiftness of his sure-footed animal, he drew his keenly polished bowie-knife in proud defiance of the danger and waved it in scorn as he rode on. It was perfectly sublime to see such super-human daring and recklessness. At each report, which came fast and thick, he kissed the flashing blade and waved it at his foes. He passed the ordeal, as awful and harrowing to a man's nerves as can be conceived, untouched by a ball and otherwise unharmed. In a few moments, a loud whoop rang out in the woods a quarter of a mile distant, and the bold rider was safe!

Joaquín, knowing well the determined character of Jim Boyce, and, deeming it more than probable that he had heard of the different large rewards offered for his capture or death amounting in the aggregate to $15,000 or $20,000, he made up his mind speedily that an attack would be made upon him by the whole party of miners if he remained at his encampment, which was some five miles distant from their tents. Concluding that they could not collect their horses together and prepare their arms and ammunition in a proper manner for an attack or pursuit before night, he conceived a plan, the most brilliant and ingenious that ever entered an outlaw's brain, by which to defeat their purposes and carry out his own original intention of robbing them. Knowing that a trail could very well be made in the night but that it could only be followed in the day-time, he ordered his men, numbering fifteen, to saddle up and make ready for a ride. They obeyed with alacrity and without question, and in a few moments were on their horses and ready to move forward. The chief led the way in silence, proceeding over the pin ridges in an easterly direction. He rode on vigorously until night over very rough ground, having traversed a distance of twenty miles; but, wishing to place a still greater distance between him and the encampment which he had left, he did not come to final halt until a late hour. Building a huge fire and hitching their animals near by, the wearied bandits hastily threw their blankets down and stretched their limbs upon them for repose. Sentinels alternately sat up until day-light, so that at the first touch of dawn the whole band arose and again started, having lost only four hours in sleep. They journeyed on in the same course as briskly as possible until noon, when, having reached a nice little valley, covered with grass and wild clover, and watered by a beautiful spring which bubbled up from the roots of a clump of evergreen oaks, distant about twenty miles from their last encampment, they stopped for two hours to let their horses graze and to refresh their own rather empty stomachs with the sardines and crackers which they generally carried with them. Here they left strong indications that they had spent the night but established the contrary fact by riding on for the remainder of the day, whose close found them at another distance of twenty miles. Building

fires as before and eating a hasty supper, they again
mounted, and, having made a circle of five miles in their
course, suddenly turned to the westward and encamped
about three o'clock, A.M., at a spot distant another common day's journey from the last starting point. Thus traveling and resting, after the lapse of a few days they found
themselves in the original trail upon which they had
started.

Jim Boyce and company had struck the path of the robbers on the next morning after their departure and had
camped each night at the fires which they had left, expect-
ing, as was natural, that they would come to a final
stopping-place when they had proceeded as far as they
liked. Joaquín smiled with exquisite satisfaction when he
perceived that Boyce was certainly ahead of him and, from
every indication, unsuspecting in the remotest degree that
his arch-enemy was at that moment in his rear.

At night, after a long day's ride over rugged mountains
and deep gulches, Jim Boyce and his company, numbering twenty-five men including himself, were seated
around one of Joaquín's late fires, which they had rekin-
dled, quietly enjoying their pipes and laughing over the
numerous stereotyped jokes,[30] which had descended, like
Shakspeare, from one gentleman to another, and are too
good ever to be worn out. The Heavens were cloudy, and
a boundary of solid darkness lay around the lighted ring
in which they sat. In the ragged clouds a few stars dimly
struggled, and the lonesome scream of the cougar, like
the wail of a lost spirit benighted in the infinity of darkness, gave a wild terror to the surrounding woods.

Suddenly and startlingly, the simultaneous reports of
fifteen pistols rent the air, the dark outer-wall of the fire-
circle blazed, as if a cloud had unbosomed its lightnings,
and the astonished survivors of the company bounded up
to see fifteen of their number stretched upon the earth

and to meet with the deadly repetition of the fifteen revolvers. Panic-stricken and bewildered, the survivors of the second discharge, numbering three men among whom was Jim Boyce, fled head-long into the darkness, and, taking no time to choose their ground, hurried madly and distractedly away from the horrible scene. Joaquín stepped quietly into the circle to see if Jim Boyce was killed, but Three-Fingered Jack leaped in like a demon with his huge knife in his mutilated hand, which had lost none of its strength, but did its three-fingered work far better than many other whole hands could do it, and soon quenched the last spark of beating life in the pale forms around him. Every one must know that death from a bullet flings a sudden and extreme paleness over the countenance, and thus the light from the fire, falling upon the ghastly faces around, displayed a sight so hideous and harrowing that Joaquín exclaimed with a shudder:

"Let's leave here, we will camp tonight, somewhere else."

Searching the bundles upon which the company had been seated, he found in different buckskin purses a sum amounting to not less than thirty thousand dollars. He also added fifteen excellent horses and ten powerful mules to his live-stock.

Jim Boyce and his surviving companions wandered to the distant settlements, which, after many hardships, they reached in safety, and it is pleasant to add that in a short time they raised another company with whom they went back to their rich diggings, and, in spite of their immense loss by Joaquín's robbery, made for themselves ample fortunes, with which they returned to the States. Should Jim Boyce chance to read this humble narrative of mine, I beg him to receive my warmest congratulations.

On one of the head-branches of the Mokelumne River,

on the last day of December, a large crowd was gathered
in and around a cloth-building in a little mining town,
which looked like a half-venture towards civilization in
the midst of that wild and savage region. A tall, dark-
skinned man sat in the middle of the room, with a huge
log-chain around one of his legs. His brow was tall and
massive, and his large, gray eyes looked forth with that
calm, cold light which unmistakably expresses a deep,
calculating intellect, divested of all feeling and independent of all motives which arise from mere impulse or
passion—an intellect which is sole in itself, looking at the
result merely in all its actions, not considering the question of right or wrong, and working out a scheme of unmitigated villainy as it would a mathematical problem.
To the right of this man sat a huge, old fellow with blue
eyes, sandy hair, and a severe look, whose scattered law-
books and papers on the table near by proclaimed him
the Justice of the Peace in that district—an office, by the
way, as important at that time in California and possessing a jurisdiction as extensive as many of the county
courts in other and older States of the Union.

The prisoner was none other than Luis Vulvia, who
had been arrested upon a charge of murder and robbery
in that town on the day before, under the following circumstances:

A German, living by himself in an isolated tent, was
heard to scream "murder!" three times; hearing which
horrible cry, five or six men some two hundred yards off
ran up to the place and at a glance comprehended the
whole scene. The German lay with his throat cut from ear
to ear and his pockets turned inside out. Looking hastily
around on the outside, they discovered two men, apparently Mexicans, who dodged on the further side of a deserted cabin and disappeared behind some rocks. Going
to the rocks and finding no further trace of the fugitives,

they went back and alarmed the whole town with a state-
ment of the circumstances. Every eye was vigilant in every
quarter, and, just as Luis Vulvia, who had observed the
fast increasing excitement, and guessed pretty nearly the
character of its cause, was mounting his horse in front of
a liquor-shop, he was suddenly knocked down with a
bludgeon, disarmed, and securely bound. The people *en
masse* securely guarded him during the night which was
just at hand, intending to hang him without a trial on the
morrow, but were dissuaded by Justice Brown, the tall,
severe-looking man above spoken of, who, being a man of
influence and a good speaker withal, convinced them that
it was better to proceed with him legally, as there was but
little doubt of his being found guilty as one of the murderers, in which case he would deliver him over to their just
vengeance. Thus the case stood up to the moment in
which the subject is introduced.

The witnesses, who ran at the cry of murder to the tent
and saw the two Mexicans dodging around the house,
could swear no further than that one of them was of
about the same size and shape as the prisoner. The bar-
keeper of the liquor-shop testified, in addition to this,
that the prisoner rode up to his door and dismounted just
a few moments before his arrest. It was well known, also,
that a dozen or more robberies had lately been committed in that neighborhood and that various persons had
met upon the roads a gang of suspicious-looking Mexicans armed to the teeth. This constituted all the testi-
mony against Vulvia, whose person was unknown to the
community, but whose name was familiar to all by repu-
tation. Had he been recognized as that noted character,
no further inquiry would have been made, but he would
have been hurried to the first convenient tree and hung
instanter. He stood on a dangerous brink. Being asked by
the Justice if he had any proof to offer in his own behalf,

he replied that he depended upon some of his acquaintances coming in during the day, who would establish his character as an honest man to the satisfaction of the court. He affirmed his innocence in a calm tone and an unflinching manner, although, could his heart have been read, he relied little upon the possibility of a rescue by his comrades, which was indeed a feeble hope, looking at the immense crowd who stood scowling upon him from every side. A silence of one-half hour rested in the court while the Justice was engaged in drawing up a transcript of the case as far as it had proceeded, when a young man superbly dressed and adorned with a splendid gold chain and watch, entered the room with gentlemanly dignity and politely addressed the Justice, to the following effect:

"My name, your Honor, is Samuel Harrington. I am a merchant and packer in the town of San José, and I am just now on my return from the more northern mines, to which I have been packing flour and other provisions. I am encamped within five miles of this place, and having heard from a citizen of your town this morning that a dark-skinned man, with gray eyes, was in custody on a charge of murder and that, although there was no positive proof against him, yet there was so strong a prejudice against Mexicans that there was great danger of his being hung by the infuriated populace, it just struck me that the prisoner might be one of my hired men, a Mexican, whom I sent into town last night, and who, much to my astonishment, did not return. I find that it is indeed the case. Your prisoner is none other than my packer and, consequently, cannot be connected with any robbing or thieving band around here. He has been with me four years, and no man ever sustained a better character. I shall wish, your Honor, to testify in his behalf, but before I take my oath, I would like to prove my identity as Mr. Harrington of San José. Please examine these letters."

He here presented to the Justice, who was already favorably impressed, five or six letters addressed in different hands to "Mr. Samuel Harrington, San José," and bearing the marks of various post offices in the State. The Justice showed these letters to several of the crowd, whose countenances immediately relaxed towards the prisoner.

"Mr. Harrington," said Squire Brown, "your evidence will be taken without a moment's scruple."

Harrington accordingly testified to the facts which he had already related, and the prisoner was discharged. Many apologies were made to Mr. H. for detaining his hired man so long, and after many compliments, he and Vulvia departed. As soon as they were clearly out of town, the both indulged in a hearty laugh.

"How came it," said Vulvia to Joaquín, "that you arrived in such good time? I had no expectation but to be hung."

"I happened to reach your camp out here in the mountains last night, having met some of our spies who guided me to it. I had not been there more than two hours before two of your men came in, and reported that they had killed a man in *that little cloth-town*, and inquired for you. Your being absent immediately created apprehension, and having waited for you anxiously till morning, we were at once convinced that you had been captured. Having most fortunately in my possession a package of letters addressed to Samuel Harrington, San José, which I had the good sense, thank God! to preserve at the time I got them into my hands, it immediately flashed on me that in case I found you arrested, I could pass myself off for a respectable merchant and so save your life. It worked to a charm as you see. I make it a practice to preserve documents of this kind, and I find that they come in pretty good play."

"But how did you come by them!" inquired Vulvia.

"Oh, easy enough. I killed a fellow on my way down here the other day and found them in his pockets—and d—d little besides, too!"

"You remind me," said Vulvia, "very much of Padre Jurata, God rest his soul! He saved many of his followers by being present at their trials, or introducing witnesses to prove an *alibi*, or presenting forged pardons on the day of execution, signed in the exact hands of the provincial governors. His knowledge was extensive, and, during his monkish life, the confessional had given him so many important and vital secrets connected with great personages that he could frequently command the services of the wealthiest men and the best-born dames of Mexico. Besides this, he sometimes officiated as one of the Fathers in the remote towns and villages."

Thus conversing, they rode on to Vulvia's camp, some ten miles in the mountains, and were met by a welcome shout from their subordinates.

While at this camp, resting his horses, Joaquín received a messenger from Reis on the Stanislaus with the news that he had killed one hundred and fifty Chinamen and had sent to the Arroyo Cantoova two hundred horses since he had last seen his chief.

"Tell him," said Joaquín, "it is all right and to go ahead; I will send him word before long. Tell him hereafter to send his horses for sake keeping to the Quien Sabe Rancho, Rancho Munos, or Joaquín Guerra's Rancho, either of the three."

Reis had managed most cunningly. Hid in an old abandoned tunnel, out of which he had whipped a gang of wolves, neither he or any of his party had been seen by day-light at all. All his thefts and robberies had been done in the night. The miserable Chinamen were mostly the sufferers, and they lay along the highways like so many sheep with their throats cut by the wolves. It was a politic stroke in Reis to kill Chinamen in preference to Americans, for no one cared for so alien a class, and they were left to shift for themselves.

One moonlight night at the hour of twelve when silence had fallen upon the world of mountains, woods, and valleys, and all quiet spirits were asleep, Reis issued from his tunnel, three hundred feet under ground, with three men, and, getting out their horses from the corral of a friendly ranchero near by—who was kind enough to take care of them, no doubt from very disinterested motives—they started on a pleasure trip up a rather lonesome road which led along a branch of the South Fork of the Stanislaus River. Coming in sight of a neat-looking frame house, Reis, bent upon an adventure, dismounted, as did also his followers, and, hitching their horses on the roadside, walked stealthily up to the house. At the first, there appeared to be a dead silence about the premises but going around on the east side, Reis discovered a light burning at a window, and, drawing nearer, heard the murmuring of voices. Not caring particularly what he did, curiosity led him to look in; which object he readily effected, being a tall man. The sight that met him was something no less ravishing than a love-scene. Upon a settee on the further side of the room, half-reclining, sat a blushing girl of seventeen years, her golden ringlets showered down upon her neck and shoulders, and her bosom heaving as if it would burst its gauzy covering and strike the gazer blind with its unspeakable loveliness. At her feet, upon the carpeted floor knelt a handsome young man, not more than twenty years of age, holding her small white hand in his, which, ever and anon, he hurried to his lips and seemed to devour it with kisses. She could not restrain his wild transports, for he caught her with a lover's fierceness around her beautiful neck and breathed his soul upon her lips. He sprang to her side and pressed her to his bosom as if he would blend his very body with her own. She looked bewildered, the beautiful creature! one moment gently striving to wrest herself from his arms, at another leaning her head upon his bosom with a sigh of unutterable love. It was a sight which might well disturb the equanimity of any man, and it is not to be wondered at that Reis looked on like one bewitched. Fate at last had some mercy on the bandit, for, after he had swallowed his up-rising heart a hundred times with looking on the enchanting beauty of the passionate girl in her lover's arms, the latter finally tore himself away and started forth from the house. One of the bandits followed him, as a matter of course, while Reis hastily concerted with the others how to act—for he was determined to abduct the beauty at all hazards.

The young man was walking very leisurely along in a bend of the road when he heard a sharp click just behind him. With sudden surprise he looked around, and there, face to face with him, stood a man, or devil, or whatever it might be, with a cocked pistol pointed within six inches of his head.

"Down on your knees or I will blow your brains out."

The young man knelt now from a different motive to that which made him kneel a short time before.

"Shell out, you dastardly scoundrel!" said the accomplished highwayman.

"There, take it," said the young man and threw his purse a few feet from him on the ground.

The robber stooped to pick it up, and, while he was bent, the young man drew a small dagger from his bootleg and plunged it into his back. It struck him directly in the spine, and the huge-bodied villain sunk without a groan.

The young man, vaguely suspecting that there might be danger lurking near his Rosalie, went back to the house. To his horror, his ears were saluted with a loud and piercing scream. Like a madman he rushed to the house, and had just entered the door of Rosalie's room and taken one glance, which showed him the terrified girl struggling in the hands of a savage-looking monster, when he was knocked senseless to the floor. The gray old mother, a lonely widow, whose only pleasure was her daughter—clung to the robber's arm and, in the trembling accents of extreme old age, beseeched him—while the tears flooded the wrinkled channels of her face—to spare her child, her only child.

"Cease your gabbling," said one of Reis' men, who knocked the old woman speechless at his feet.

"Who told you to do that?" said Reis and instantly shot the officious scoundrel through the heart.

"Now, my pretty duck, you can come along with me," he said, turning to his captive.

But at the sight of the ruffian's blow, which felled her mother, Rosalie's blue eyes had closed in a swoon, and paleness, as of death, had overspread her features.

"It makes no difference," said Reis to his surviving companion, "she will soon get over it, anyhow; let us go along."

"I don't know that I care about going just now," the cut-throat replied, looking as black as a thunder-cloud, "after what you have done to poor Francisco there," laying his hand on his pistol at the same time.

"You don't, eh!" said Reis, drawing his revolver, "then you are as trifling a scoundrel as he is."

The two fired at once; the subordinate fell dead, and Reis was grazed on his right cheek with a piece of hot lead, which made him blush, if his own villainy did not.

"Blast the two miserable scoundrels," said he, "it actually seems as if some men had no humanity at all."

Tying the rounded wrists of his lovely, drooping captive with his handkerchief, he proceeded to the spot where the horses were hitched, cut them loose, all but his own, and mounted into his saddle with his precious booty before him. The loosened horses dashed back to the corral from which they had been taken, and Reis rode on by himself till within a quarter of a mile of his tunnel, when he got down with his now weeping burden, turned his horse loose, which followed the others, and proceeded on foot at his leisure.

Rosalie begged him to release her with so much sorrowful sweetness in her voice, with so beautiful an agony expressive in her whole enchanting form that the rocky-hearted Reis almost repented of what he had done.

"It won't do," he thought, "to let her go now, for I will have nothing to show for my night's work, and how should I account to the band for the missing members?"

"You sha'n't be hurt," said he, turning mildly towards the trembling maiden, "I am going to keep you only a few days until I can get a ransom for you, which some of your friends will no doubt pay, when you send them word by one of our number."

They soon reached the entrance of the tunnel into which he dragged the shuddering girl and led her, half-dead with terror, into the extreme end, where sat his fierce-looking companions in a well-lighted apartment.

The bandits, much interested, gathered around their captain, who informed them—:

"That he had attacked a certain house on the road and succeeded in entering, but found no money, which disappointed him so much that he took this very beautiful girl in the place of it;" and further stated, "that in the struggle at the house, two of his men were killed before his face, and one was missing, he being probably killed, as well as the others. As for this handsome girl," he concluded, "we may as well keep her for a ransom, or one of us may marry her, just as we see fit."

Poor, poor Rosalie! may Heaven protect you, for man cannot.

Rosalie, on the second night after her capture, resolved to help herself. Rising from a warm couch of blankets already dressed, and unperceived by the bandits, who lay slumbering around, she started into the throat of the tunnel in order to find her way out. Pressing her hand to her heart to still its loud beatings, she stepped noiselessly along until she had left the sleeping apartment, when looking forward, she saw that every light in front of her had been extinguished. Pausing with indefinable dread at the thought of walking that fearful passage alone, she heard a loud yawn from one of the sleepers as if he were waking, and with a sudden movement, which was scarce voluntary, she shot like an arrow into the blackness which lay before her. On and on and on she moved with trembling footsteps, feeling her way on the sides of the tunnel and placing her feet each time with the indescribable terrible feeling that she might be stepping off into some deep abyss below. It seemed ages to her before she could reach the entrance. Oh, that she might but catch one friendly glimpse of light! It appears—a faint, flickering gleam in the distance. With hurrying feet she approaches—larger and larger it grows until she sees the lamp, like a full-blown rose of light, swinging from the arch, joy! her escape is certain. She stands now in the full blaze, she sees no one, and, with a more confident heart, pursues her way. She was now near the entrance. She saw the moonlight flooding the world without and rushed eagerly forward. A huge figure started suddenly before her, and the beautiful girl fainted. It was a bad time to swoon, but how could so delicate an organization, fit only to be played upon by the subtlest flashes of thought, sporting in rainbow-fancies, sustain so rude a shock? She fell gasping for breath, and the sentinel, for it was he, carried her to the apartment which she had left, and tenderly laid her upon her couch without disturbing any one in the room, and hurried back to his post.

So tenderly delicate was this innocent creature, so divine the appealing spirit of her eyes as she looked into his face, that Reis could not find it in his heart to treat her with anything but the profoundest respect. He had seized her in a moment of passion, stung with her voluptuous beauty, and would at that moment have fought for her as for a conquest of so much of Heaven itself. Such is the maddening effect of beauty upon the hearts of men! But on sober reflection, he banished the vain idea which he had been foolish enough to vaguely entertain that she could ever love a man like him, rude and uncouth as he was, and seriously contemplated restoring her to her aged and widowed mother, and one whom he knew that she loved. Confused and tormented with doubt, she was a continual trouble on his hands. He was not scoundrel enough to force her into a vile position, and he was afraid to leave her for a moment in the hands of his less scrupulous comrades. Already had they began to murmur at him for his weakness, and he had been forced to threaten some of their lives, if they did not keep their distance from the girl. There was danger of a mutiny, and so critical was his situation that, notwithstanding he dreaded Joaquín's opinion of his conduct in this specific matter, yet he longed to see him.

Reis was sitting one night, moping in his tunnel like a grim wolf and scowling discontentedly around him, for he had done nothing for a week, when the sentinel came in, attended by two persons whom he left standing before Reis, and returned to his post. The melancholy bandit raised his head and beheld his now dreaded chief before him. Joaquín glanced hastily around the room and, beholding the captive girl reclining mournfully upon her couch, he started, and with a sudden fierceness which made every man in his presence quail, turned to Reis, and said with a look that rived his soul—:

"How is this? Did I ever instruct you to engage in a business of this kind? Explain yourself, or by G—d, it will not be well for you."

Reis begged him to listen patiently and related every circumstance connected with the girl's capture, his killing his two comrades at the time, and everything which followed subsequently.

Joaquín was in a tempest of anger.

"So you have done nothing but mope for the past week—essential service you have rendered to our organization. Reis," he continued, convulsively clutching his pistol-handle, "if it was any other man but you, I would kill him on the spot. I would shoot him like a dog. But d—n you," he exclaimed with sudden vehemence, while his eyes blazed as none but his could, "have you done her any injury? Have you taken any advantage of that girl, sir?"

"No, no. You know I would scorn to do that," replied Reis.

"I believe you, and it is well that it is so. Reis," he continued, in a calmer tone, "I am surprised at you. *I* have never done a thing of this kind. I have higher purposes in view than to torture innocent females. I would have no woman's person without her consent. I have read of robbers who deliberately ravished tender and delicate females and, afterwards, cut their throats, but I despise them. I am no such robber, and I never will be. Reis—I *ought* to kill you, but since you have had *some* honor and manhood about you in this rascally matter, I will let you off this time. Get you in readiness, and we will, you and

I alone, return this girl to her mother, if the poor, old woman be alive, and forthwith set this matter right. I wouldn't at such a time as this be bothered by a frivolous matter of this kind for all the women in the world, spread out in a perfect sea of bosoms and lips!"

Rosalie, who had been listening with intense interest to every word, at this moment sprang towards the young chief, whose appearance was far from forbidding even to the most refined female, and, in a fit of uncontrollable gratitude and rapture at the prospect of her deliverance, threw her arms around his neck before she thought. Recovering herself instantly, she thanked him in a dignified manner for his noble conduct and told him that she respected him from the bottom of her heart, robber as he was.

Joaquín looked at her proudly, as he laid his hand upon his breast, and said:

"Yes, Senorita, I *am* a man. I was once as noble a man as ever breathed, and if I am not so now, it is because men would not allow me to be as I wished. You shall return to your mother and to your lover, if I die in bringing it about."

On this same night at eleven o'clock, stood the frame house on the road that leads up on a branch of the South Fork of the Stanislaus River, the same as it was on that happy, sorrowful night when Rosalie was embraced by her lover and torn from his presence. In one of the rooms sat her old, disconsolate mother, whose withering life was alone sustained by the hope of seeing her daughter again, and near her the young man Edward—. He was comforting the old lady with assurances, which did not quiet his own heart, for he had ridden day and night over one-half of the county, making inquiries in every quarter, but not a trace could he find of the missing girl or her abductor. His face was pale and thin with anxiety, and his voice had something hollow in it, as though the vampire

of despair was sucking his heart's blood. He began to believe that his adored Rosalie was lost to him forever and
was doomed to a fate he could not contemplate without a
shuddering chill. After soothing the feeble brain of the
old woman with what he knew to be the merest illusions,
he had subsided into silence, and was eating his heart in
bitter regret when a sudden tap was heard on the door
and, in a moment, leaped into the room the very object of
his thoughts. The meeting was such as might be expected.
But I will not fill this sheet with an attempt at a description of it: Edward's rapture, astonishment, bewilderment
of joy!—the old decrepid mother's scarce audible sylla-
bles and her far more expressive tears. Rapidly was her
story recounted by Rosalie, and with such enthusiasm
did she dwell on the heroic conduct of Joaquín that her
lover almost became jealous of the young robber. She
made him swear that he would never injure *that man*,
whatever he might do to others.

"I won't touch Joaquín," he replied, "if he lets me
alone, but as for that other bloody beast, I will kill him
the first time I lay my eyes on him."

Joaquín at this moment walked in and stood before the
young man. Reis very prudently remained on the outside,
after hearing the observation which had just been made re-
specting him.

"I have done you a favor, sir," said Joaquín, "and now I
want you to keep this matter a profound secret. Never
breathe my name out of this house. I will be in this county
for some time, but you and yours shall not be troubled. But
if you betray me, I will scatter to the winds all that you
have and all that you love."

"It is hard," said the young man "to be under obligations to a man like you, but I will be silent."

"And who are *you*, pray, that talk as if it were stooping
to be under obligations to a man like me?" and the fiery

spirit of Joaquín leaped into his eyes. He touched the hilt of his bowie-knife, when a supplicating look from Rosalie checked him.

Edward —— drew his revolver half out, but Rosalie touched his arm, and, with a reproachful look, said to him:

"Fie, fie, Edward, you forget yourself. You wouldn't harm the man who has restored me to your arms? Why, Edward, would you make me despise you? I care not if he were a robber a thousand times, he is a noble man— shake hands with him," and, taking his with her left and the robber's with her right, she joined them together with a gentle force.

Sternly, the young men looked at each other for a second, and then, with a half-friendly, half-defiant smile, they parted.

Joaquín and Reis rode off, the one somewhat more reconciled to his subordinate, since the issue had been good, and the other delighted beyond all bounds at the happy turn which things had taken.

"I would have given her up long ago," exclaimed Reis, "but my men would have killed me for it, I am certain. It was fortunate that you came when you did, or the poor girl would have been far worse off than she is now, the beautiful creature that she is!" said he, with enthusiasm.

Rosalie and Edward —— were shortly after married. They kept their secret while Joaquín lived, and, for my part, I do not blame them.

The new year opened, the ever memorable year of 1853, and, by the middle of January, the bold and accomplished bandit was ready to enter upon a series of the bloodiest scenes that ever were enacted in the same space of time in any age or country. Calaveras County, as I have said before—the richest, or among the richest at least, in the Golden State—he chose as the theater of his operations, and never was a region so scourged and desolated. Detached parties numbering four, five, or a dozen men were scattered over the face of the whole country, and so diverse were their operations, so numerous and swift, that I shall not attempt to give a minute account of them but shall confine myself particularly to the individual movements of Joaquín and strictly to those facts which are absolutely known and traceable to their original source. It may be distinctly set down, however, in the outset, that though many villainous deeds which transpired in the short period which I am about to make a sketch of were mysterious and unaccountable, many murders committed in parts remote from each other, robberies here, thefts there, and destruction, lightening-footed, treading everywhere, invisible in its approach and revealed only in the death-trail which it left behind, yet all this mighty and seemingly chaotic scene had its birth in the dramatic brain of Joaquín—an author who acted out his own tragedies! Divergent as were the innumerable lines of action, yet they were all concentrated upon one point and directed to one purpose—that which existed in the breast of Joaquín.

There was not a town of any importance in that whole region in which he had not a spy, one or more, located; not one in which he had not his agents and secret friends. He lacked not for harboring-places in which to conceal his wounded men and stolen animals. I might here mention numerous ranchos, owned by wealthy and respectable men (as the world goes) which afforded him refuge and assistance when needed, but, for fear that they may have since changed hands, I will, for the present, spare them.

Around San Andreas, Calaveritas, and Yackee Camp, numerous thefts and robberies had been committed for several weeks past. Property was missed, but no one knew whither it was gone. Men were murdered, and the bloody hand remained unseen. Yet every one knew that thieves and murderers walked unknown in the midst of the community. A strange dread hung over every face and gave vigilance to every eye. The fearful shrunk back from a danger which they could *feel* but not see. The bold stood forward with their lives in their hands to search into, find, and face the perils which existed around them, the more terrible that they were disguised and concealed. Among the boldest, most firm, and energetic whom the crisis brought forth was Capt. Charles H. Ellas of San Andreas, who, in his capacity of deputy sheriff of Calaveras County, took the lead in ferreting out the perpetrators of these foul deeds. He was a young man of fine appearance, slenderly formed, but making up for the want of superior strength in great activity and astonishing powers of endurance. His eyes were keen, quick, and flashing, touched with a fierceness which at times seemed to scorch where it fell. A chivalrous son of the South, he had grown up under a discipline which taught him that honor was a thing to be maintained at the sacrifice of blood or of life itself; that fear was a feeling too base to harbor in a manly breast, and that *he* was a coward who would not give the question of his rights to the arbitration of steel or of the deadly ball. Already did his bosom bear the marks of severe and dangerous hand-to-hand conflicts, a trial of muscle, nerve, and skill in a game whose stake is human life and whose hazard is eternity.

At a juncture so important as the period of which I speak, a man like Ellas was most naturally looked to as a leader and intrusted with a large amount of discretionary power, so necessary to be used in perilous times when the slow forms of law, with their snail-like processes, are altogether useless and inefficient.

The first opportunity which presented itself for anything like determinate action occurred about the middle of January. Some horses were stolen at the town of San Andreas, and a description of the Mexicans who took them had been given to Capt. Ellas, who, in the course of a day's ride on the various roads, accidentally discovered the party on the road leading from Yackee Camp to Chaparral Hill. They had added two to their number, who were not perceived, however, by the Captain at the first glance. Seeing two mounted men on a small hill to the left of the road, he hailed them and requested them to come down, as he had something to say. One of them replied:

"If you want to see us more than we do you, come to us."

Whereupon Ellas advanced, but the intermediate space being marshy, much rain having lately fallen, his mare mired so badly that he dismounted. Proceeding on foot, he heard a rustling in the brush to the right, which sounded very much like an ambush ready to burst forth, but he kept on his way. When within eighty yards of the two to whom he had spoken, he saw that they had drawn their revolvers. This hostile movement and the rustling in the brush to the right convinced him that he was acting a very imprudent part and that he was even then in very imminent danger. With much presence of mind, he looked behind him and gave a signal-whistle as if he had a company in waiting, which stratagem succeeded so well that the two in open sight rode slowly over the hill, and those who had been concealed, precipitately left the thicket. Going to where his mare was feeding, he mounted her and went over to Yackee Camp, a little mining town a few miles distant, in order to get men to go out with him in further pursuit. He found no one at all prepared to accompany him but a Mexican merchant in the place named Atanacio Moreno, a man who was worth money, and stood well in the community. Unsuspected by Ellas, this man secretly belonged to the band of Joaquín Murieta, or, I should rather say, to the tremendous organization which

that bold chieftain had established throughout the country. The Captain had unlimited confidence in this individual, for he had previously assisted him in the capture of a
horse-thief, and, besides giving him much valuable information, had furnished men and horses in various expeditions started by the honest portion of the community.

He was treacherous, and, though assisting to capture
individuals, sometimes, who belonged to his own fraternity, they were always those whom he hated personally.
A dangerous companion in a lonely ride! Moreno, claim-
ing to have watched through his spies the movements of
the depredators, led the way over the mountains, valleys,
and gulches until sunset, but no trace of the objects
sought was found, and the pursuit was here relinquished.

It became known before a great while, for a certainty,
that this man was a scoundrel, and, leaving the country
in a few weeks after his connection with Joaquín was discovered, he joined *Senati*,[31] a petty robber of some note in
the south. He had not been with that leader long before
he secretly assassinated him, cut off his head, and delivered it to the civil authorities of the town of Los Angeles
for a reward of five hundred dollars, which had been offered for it. This act of treachery did not avail him much,
for he was afterwards arrested on a grave charge and
thrown into prison, where he now lies, and it is only
owing to the delay of the law that he is not already hung.

It was soon ascertained that an organized band of robbers was in the community of San Andreas. Yackee Camp
was discovered to be their rendezvous, situated about
two miles and a half from San Andreas. Upon this discovery, Capt. Ellas employed a number of spies to gather
all the information that they could in relation to the
thieves and robbers, whose leader was not then known.
While these spies were out, Capt. Ellas one day rode into
Yackee Camp, and was seated on his horse near a little

drinking-house, observing matters and things in that very suspicious vicinity, when he perceived a young, black-eyed, fine-looking fellow, standing with his cloak wrapped around him, very intently fixing his gaze upon himself. As soon as their eyes met, the young fellow drew the rim of his hat over his face, and, flinging his cloak a little back from his shoulder, dropped his arm down carelessly toward the butt of his pistol. In a moment more, he turned and walked off. Capt. Ellas will no doubt recollect the circumstance, and must not be surprised to learn that this was none other than Joaquín himself, who thus took his daguerreotype upon memory and found it afterwards of much avail in aiding him to escape danger, and to keep out of the way when he saw the original at the head of an armed party, or otherwise to direct his movements to the best advantage. The Captain did not, this time, even know Joaquín was in the county, although the renowned robber's name was familiar to his ears by the report of his depredations in other counties, for a long time back. The spies, after the lapse of several days, returned with the information that they had discovered several lurking-places of the robbers, among which was Chaparral Hill, a description of which it may be as well to give, inasmuch as it was the scene of quite an interesting event. It lies to the southwest of San Andreas about four miles, and is nothing more than an elevated pass between two steep ridges, which are crowned with precipitous rocks whose interstices would effectually conceal a man from observation. Thickets of chaparral cover various spots on the tops of the ridges, with open spaces between, and, in many places, the live-oak trees, with low branches and crooked, knotty trunks, form a kind of natural fortification, almost as perfect as if they had been arranged expressly for the purpose. The pass itself is but a lowering of a long curving wall, (a natural wall) which connects the two ridges together, and, between these ridges, a long hollow leads up and terminates at the pass. By the foot of the hollow runs a clear little stream margined with green grass, called Willow Creek, because it is fringed so beautifully with the lithe and graceful trees of that name. Behind the curving wall described, a steep descent goes down to the valley below, and is covered with immense greasewood thickets, taller than a man's head, through which a party pursued could make a most safe retreat and through which it would be dangerous to follow them. A few tall pines stand isolated, here and there, on the different eminences, which shoot up in rugged majesty from the general outline. One ridge terminates at the connecting wall, but the other stretches on a mile or two beyond it, marked by a bridle-trail which suddenly plunges into a succession of deep ravines and gulches lined with greasewood and low timber—lonely, and sombre-looking places! From this pass, or any place adjacent, a view of the country is commanded many miles in extent.

A few days after the return of the spies, a gentleman by the name of Hall, who kept a rancho on the road leading from Mokelumne Hill to San Andreas, called on Ellas and informed him that three Mexicans had passed his house that morning who looked suspicious, they having but two horses and one of the men in consequence mounted behind another. One of these men had been detained by him at his house, having stopped but a few moments while the others rode on but remained no longer than he saw fit, after all, for, upon the first movement towards preventing his free agency, he drew a revolver and walked out. Hall and a man named Davis followed the party about a mile and saw where they had left the main road and gone up Murray's Creek.

Ellas mounted his horse, accompanied by his friend, a young lawyer of fine parts by the name of Wm. J. Latewood who had practiced at squirrels and turkies in the woods as much as he had practiced at the bar, and was as skillful in drawing a "bead" as in drawing a brief—and attended also by Hall, Davis, and another man whose name is not remembered—Hall being provided with a pistol, Davis with a rifle, and the other man with a yager.[32] The party numbered five, hastily gotten up, and but poorly prepared for a combat; but, supposing that he was only on the track of three Mexicans, the Captain proceeded on their trail. Immediately after starting, he met a gentleman named Peter Woodbeck, whom, having a little business with, he requested to ride back a short distance with the company. Arriving at Murray's Creek, he struck a fresh trail of two horses, as expected, about a mile from San Andreas, leading behind a ridge of mountains that skirted that little town—showing that the riders had kept themselves concealed from view of the main road until immediately opposite San Andreas, at which point they had evidently ridden to the top of the ridge and who, no doubt, saw their pursuers start out and, at the same time, counted their number. The trail from this point led over the mountains towards Yackee Camp, which gave Ellas to suppose they were a part of the band said to be lurking about Chaparral Hill. He immediately sent Peter Woodbeck to San Andreas with a request to Alcalde[33] Taliaferro to send two parties of men, each numbering five, and have them stationed on the different trails leading from the Chaparral Hill. The Alcalde, being sick, was unable to attend personally to the request, but used every exertion in his power by his agents to raise the two parties needed—unfortunately, without success. Under the impression that the men would be stationed as desired, the

Captain rode on. The trail wound along in a very circuitous manner over the roughest possible places so that it was in the afternoon before he reached the foot of the hollow before spoken of, at Willow Creek, only four miles from San Andreas. Ascending the hollow, the pursuing party immediately saw, on the curve of the pass of Chaparral Hill, several Mexicans mounted upon fine horses and rode up towards them until within rifle-shot, when they halted. Two or three of the Mexicans rode down behind some bushes and rocks on the slant and commenced firing at them with Colt's heavy pistols, but without effect. Ellas and party immediately shifted their position to a place within fair pistol-shot, during which movement Davis levelled his rifle at a fellow partially hid in the rocks and evidently hit him. The man with the yager in vain tried to fire it—it would not "go off," and the weapon remained useless through the whole fight, as well as the bearer of it, who had nothing else with which to do battle. Though sadly needed, he stood neutral as far as any service he could do was concerned but served admirably well as a target for the bandits to practice at, nevertheless. To aggravate the state of things, Davis, after discharging his rifle, could find no more bullets in his pouch, and was thus also rendered unable to do anything. Only three men therefore were left to do the fighting! The Mexicans, noticing this dilemma, dashed along on the curve of the hill, nine in number, splendidly mounted, and well-armed; some were observed to have two revolvers apiece. While passing, they fired about twenty shots, but were riding so rapidly that they could not shoot with precision. As it was, Gatewood's mule was severely wounded in the neck, and bled profusely. A ball passed across Ellas's breast, burning a hole in the side of his vest, and another went through his hair. After this swoop of theirs, they retired to their first position. A portion of them, then dismounting, crept down behind the bushes, so as to get near enough to Ellas's party to make a dead shot, and commenced firing but not with the desired certainty, for Ellas and Gatewood had dismounted, and were somewhat protected by their animals. The Captain, finding an opportunity for the first time to fire with any chance of hitting, shot at a large Mexican who stood on the edge of a bush, who suddenly retired to the top of the hill. Upon the report of his pistol, his mare, a fine, well-trained animal, went down the hollow about four hundred yards towards Willow Creek, upon which one of the mounted Mexicans dashed around as if to secure her. She ran back towards Ellas, and the Mexican followed to within seventy yards, immediately below him. Ellas fired, and the fellow sunk on the neck of his horse, apparently badly wounded. Four or five of the Mexicans, noticing this, galloped along the ridge towards the side of the hill to which the wounded Mexican had retired and effectually covered his position, so that it was impossible to approach him without receiving their fire. He was then wrapping his red scarf around his breast, as if endeavoring to stop the blood. Ellas's horse soon dashed to the left of the Mexicans and came to him, when he mounted and led his party around towards the right hand ridge in order to gain the summit, if possible, which object he hoped to effect while the opposing force was somewhat separated. In passing under a steep rocky place, Gatewood exclaimed, "There is a Mexican above us," and had scarcely finished the sentence before the fellow commenced firing with his revolver. He fired three distinct shots at a distance of not more than forty yards. Ellas suddenly wheeled his horse, discovered him almost perpendicularly over his head, not more than thirty yards distant, mounted upon a white horse; and, taking a steady aim with his six-shooter, pulled the trigger. The Mexican fell back upon his saddle, wounded in the breast, but, soon recovering himself, put spurs to his horse and darted out of sight. Up to this time, the Captain had concluded to risk this very disadvantageous battle in the hope that the two parties sent by Peter Woodbeck would arrive on the two trails in the rear of the robbers; but finding that they were not likely to come, and knowing that he was exposing himself and comrades to be shot down in detail from behind the rocks and bushes, he decided to retire to the foot of the hollow where his opponents could not assail him without exposure to themselves. They did not follow him, and after a short consultation with his comrades, he started back for San Andreas, which he reached without difficulty and immediately proceeded to organize a party. While doing this, word came from Yackee Camp that six men (evidently of the same band) had come down into that place from the direction of Chaparral Hill, and, without a moment's parley, had commenced killing the few Americans with whom they happened to meet. Joaquín (for it was with him that Ellas had been fighting, without knowing it) rode among the houses during the shooting and remarked:

"This is not my fight—this is Bill's fight," alluding to an affray between one of his friends named Bill, who was a Mexican gambler in the place, and some Americans, which had occurred a short time before.

When this remark was made, Three-Fingered Jack discharged his pistol at an American, who was standing near, and killed him on the spot. Another American, whom Joaquín recognized, started to run; he was on foot, but ran with as much speed over the rough ground, which had been dug up and ditched in various places by the miners, as did the robber-chief, who pursued him on horseback. Leaping and plunging through the holes and ditches,

Joaquìn shot at him six times without effect, and, having thus emptied his "six-shooter," finally threw at him his two-edged sword, which barely missed the poor fellow's neck just as he escaped in a ledge of rocks. It was a trying scene for any man to pass through and of a character such as he would not soon forget. Joaquín reloaded his revolver, recovered his sword, and rode back into town, swearing that he would get even on that day's work if it took him twenty years, for he had lost three of his best men on Chaparral Hill.

"God damn that little Sheriff of San Andreas," said he, "I knew him all the time!"

Soon after, having cleared out of the Americans in Yackee Camp, he galloped off with his men, numbering six, over the hills towards the mountains, leaving one wounded horse, which had been shot in the late skirmish at the pass.

Upon receiving this information, Ellas started for Yackee Camp with his party, consisting of six mounted men, followed by some thirty citizens of San Andreas on foot. Arriving at the tragical scene, they immediately seized the Mexican gambler Bill, who had been foolish enough to remain after Joaquín's remark about him, and, having subjected him to a California trial,[34] they sentenced him to be hung "forthwith" as a member of Joaquín's band. He begged them earnestly to spare his life, but, finding it was in vain, his brow darkened, and, with an air of proud defiance, he told them to do their work.

"By going to my trunk," said he, "you will find a knife, from whose blade no handkerchief has yet wiped the d—d American blood."

This speech did not serve to mollify the state of feeling toward him, and he was jerked up into a tree, and strangled with very little ceremony.

It was now a late hour in the night, but there remained

a finishing stroke to be put upon the proceedings before retiring to rest. The harboring places and dens of the robbers were found out, and the enraged citizens went to work tearing down and burning up the houses of this character. The conflagration lit up the vault of Heaven, and its sound roared among the mountains for miles around. Joaquín saw and heard it with a laugh.

"If they could only throw *us* into it now," said he, "it would be fine."

Around the smouldering ruins, guards and pickets were stationed till morning, and the wearied citizens slept. At daylight, three companies were organized, two mounted and one on foot, whose object was to break up the whole confederacy of robbers and their harborers and never to rest until the neighborhood was free from them. A man named Henry Scroble took charge of one mounted company, and Ellas of the other. The former proceeded over the mountains, and Ellas over the lower hills in a different direction. At the Phenix Quartz Mill, a few miles from Yackee Camp, he and his party were shocked to see two dead bodies, lying mutilated with knives and bullets. The building was perforated in various places with balls, a dead horse with a bullet hole in his side lay near by, and everything bore evidence of a hard fight. One of the murdered men was Peter Woodbeck, who had been marked by the robbers when Ellas sent him back with word to Alcalde Taliaferro. The brave fellow had fought like a true American, long and well, but who can prevail against a league of men and devils in an evil hour? The shot which killed the horse might have saved Woodbeck's life had it been aimed a little higher; so trivial are the circumstances which often determine the fortunes of men!

The trail of the murderers from Quartz Mill was plain, leading over the San Domingo Creek range of mountains, following which Ellas and company met with the foot company, which had been detailed to go through the rougher part of the mountainous section near the Cherokee Flat. They gave him some interesting information which was that they had found clothing which had evidently been thrown from a wounded man and, upon the discovery, had proceeded immediately to a camp not far off where they found two Mexicans, one of them badly wounded. The sound one rose to his feet and started at full speed, but was shot, so that he died a short time afterwards in an adjacent thicket to which he ran before he fell. This individual was not a "fighting member," but rather a sly and secret friend who had volunteered to take care of one of Joaquín's wounded men who had been hit in the skirmish at Chaparral Hill the day before. They also saw, in a neighboring thicket of chaparral, three other mounted men of the robber-band, whom they did not find an opportunity to attack. The wounded man was still lying at the camp, unable to get out of the way without help. It was dark when Ellas received this information, but, determined to lose no opportunity of meeting with the scoundrels, he stationed men around the chaparral thickets to watch during the night, sent others to arrest the wounded robber at the camp and to convey him to Cherokee Flat,[35] and hurried off two others to two different ferries on the Stanislaus River, with orders to the ferrymen to allow no one to cross. The wounded man being a trouble upon their hands, and, no doubt, being entertained as to his character, the Cherokee half-breeds and others at the Cherokee House concluded to hang him, a very necessary ceremony which was soon performed.

Ellas lay watching the camp from which the wounded robber had been taken, all night, in the hope that some of his companions might come; but none arrived. Early in the morning, he gathered his party and started on a bush-trail over the Bear Mountain, scaling its highest point. In several places along this trail, he found spots where men had manifestly stopped and thrown up clotted blood from their stomachs. Tracking on, he reached a Chinese camp, which the Chinamen informed them had just been robbed by three Mexicans who took their last cent and barely allowed them to escape with their lives. Hurrying forward from here, he found that they had crossed the river at Forman's Rancho, despite all efforts to prevent them. Upon the other side, they struck the main road which led along its banks, and their distant trail was lost among the number of tracks common to a public highway. On the next day, still indefatigably searching through the woods, he again found their trail which conducted him within a mile of San Andreas, and was again lost in the main road. All trace of them was then lost for three or four days at the expiration of which, as the Captain was riding along with three followers, a friendly Mexican named Jesus Ahoa came up to him and informed him that he had noticed some Mexicans leading horses over a mountain near Greaserville on the Calaveras River, who looked exceedingly suspicious. Following Jesus Ahoa as a guide, Ellas and his three comrades rode to the mountain indicated and very readily fell upon the trail. Proceeding a few miles, they found three horses which had been left lariated on the way in a sequestered spot between two steep ridges. Further on, they met two or three Americans, who had seen Joaquín and two others pass them not a great while before, riding at full speed down the river, Joaquín being mounted on a thoroughbred American mare. Ellas, with his usual energy, diligently pursued their trail until the dusk of the evening when he arrived at an isolated drinking-house, whose inmates refused to give any information whatever concerning the pursued party. The trail was, however, yet visible, and led down to the bank of the Calaveras River, which he crossed, finding the trail again without much difficulty. It ran up the river a short distance and re-crossed it. The Captain did the same and found it again upon the first bank. It led out a short distance towards Angel's Camp, a little mining town a few miles off, but doubled upon itself again, and again crossed the river. It was now dark and impossible to find the lost trail, even if it had been practicable to follow it when found. The pursuit was, accordingly, given up for that night. The next morning, the Captain rode up to an isolated house in a wild section of the mountains, where lived a rough-looking Mexican, solitary and alone, and discovered at his door the tracks of several horses, which he knew were the same horses that had made the trail of the day before, from the peculiarity in one of the hoofs which was very distinctly impressed at every step. The ill-looking fellow denied all knowledge of any mounted men having been to his house. A lariat was speedily attached to his neck, and he was sent up into a tree to see if he could not obtain the desired information. Having been sent up twice, he ascertained the important fact that Joaquín had passed his house the night before with two other men and had told him that he was going to Campo Seco, on his way to the city of Marysville in the northern country—that the neighborhood was getting too warm for him, and he wanted a little fresh air—that he intended to return, for he would never rest satisfied until he had the heart's blood of Ellas and the Mexican who had put the Captain on his trail, etc.

The next day after this the Captain ascertained that Joaquín had crossed the Stanislaus River at Lancha Plano with his party, forcing the ferrymen to act contrary to orders and put him over. He had scarcely landed on the other side before he was attacked by a party of Americans, (for it must be borne in mind that the whole country was aroused) who, being superior in number, poured hot lead into his midst with such bewildering rapidity that he was compelled to fly with the utmost precipitation, leaving, in his hurry, several very fine, loose horses. It was supposed that he soon after swam the river at another place, and was still in the neighborhood. Accompanied by a gentleman from Angel's Camp, Ellas went to the fastnesses of the Bear Mountain Range in the hope to discover fresh trails; found one which led towards a camp called Los Muertos; the tracks indicating that there were five mounted men. Being in no condition to follow them, he rode over to Cherokee Flat and requested a number of Cherokees, located there, to go out and way-lay the different trails between Bear Mountain and San Domingo Range, to which they readily assented. In the meantime, a meeting was held at Carson's Creek of the citizens to take measures in the pressing exigency, which was upon that district in common with others. A Mexican was noticed in the meeting attentively observing its proceedings, who, as soon as it broke up, was seen to go to a bakery, purchase a quantity of bread, and start off on foot in the direction of Bear Mountain. He was followed and seized on the side of the mountain, and, at the same time, his captors discovered three Mexicans riding on the ridge a few hundred yards above them. One of these was Joaquín, and the others were Reis and Valenzuela. The captive Mexican was hurried away to Cherokee Flat, where he was questioned closely in regard to his conduct. He played the part of an idiot, and would have succeeded in convincing the attendant crowd that he was really a poor imbecile, had he not been very well known by some of "the boys." To bring him to his senses, hemp was suggested as a very efficacious thing in such cases, and he was, accordingly, elevated into the top of a tree to take a view of the surrounding country. The remedy operated upon his ailment like a charm, and he confessed without hesitation that he knew Joaquín, Reis, Valenzuela, and numerous others of the banditti; and that Joaquín was at this time not far off, to whom he was taking provisions when he was apprehended. A doubt arising in the minds of some persons, not noted for decision of character, as to whether it was right to put the fellow to death, Ellas left him in charge of the two Cherokee half-breeds with the request that they would give a good account of him, whereupon the crowd dispersed. At about twelve o'clock in the night, the Cherokees went to Ellas's house in San Andreas and informed him that they were ready to give "a good account" of the Mexican. Nothing more was said on the subject, and the next day, he was found hanging on a tree by the side of the road.

Several weeks had now transpired since the fight on Chaparral Hill, and, notwithstanding the most diligent pursuit having been made after the robbers, yet during the whole time they had been busily engaged in murder, theft, and plunder. They left a broad and bloody trail wherever they went and committed their outrages, at times, in the very sight of their pursuers. Frequently were the harrowing cries of "murder" heard just ahead, and, hastening to the spot, citizens were found weltering in their blood while the audacious bandits were seen riding off with no great evidence of fear at being overtaken. The banditti were divided, the greater portion of the time, into small companies of four or five, and Joaquín was seldom seen with more than three followers. Three-Fingered Jack was his constant attendant. Vulvia was in the field; Reis was active; and Valenzuela was far from idle.

On the fifth of February, a Mexican was arrested by the citizens at Angel's Camp. As soon as it was done, a young Sonorian gambler ran to a horse hitched at a rack, and was preparing to mount, no doubt to carry information to Joaquín of what had transpired, when a pistol was cocked in his face, and he was stopped. In a few moments, it was ascertained that the man arrested was one of Joaquín's band, and he soon made his exit into eternity from the branch of an oak tree, which yet stands at Angel's Camp as one of its memorials.

Three or four Germans, sleeping in a tent on a rather lonesome ravine near to Angel's Creek a few nights before the event last mentioned, were surprised to find themselves suddenly tied, hand and foot, in their beds and still more horrified when a scowling band of ruffians stood over them with drawn sabres, which they drew across their throats so carelessly that it started the blood. The Germans eagerly delivered up what money they had, which amounted to the pitiful sum of two hundred dollars; at which Three-Fingered Jack, for he was there with his leader, jumped up with an oath that made the poor fellows quiver where they lay and declared that he would dig their hearts out of them for not having any more, suiting his act to the word by brandishing his knife over their heads and waving it to and fro within an inch of their windpipes. Joaquín, however, interfered and prevented him from executing his threat, remarking that it was better to let them live as he might wish to collect taxes off of them for "Foreign Miners' Licenses,"[36] at some other time.

One Alexander Bidenger and his friend, G. J. Mansfield, residing at a little place called Capulope, having learned from two friendly Mexicans that Joaquín had slept there on the night of the second of February, with other important information, concluded to send word to Justice Beatty, the presiding magistrate at Campo Seco, not a great way off, and, having written a letter, dispatcher it by "Digger-Express."[37]

To those unacquainted with California customs, it may

be necessary to explain that it is common in the mountains and mining districts to employ Digger Indians as bearers of letters, or runners upon errands, from one point to another, they being very expeditious on foot and willing to travel a considerable distance for a small piece of bread, fresh meat, or a ragged shirt. I have known them to swim rivers when the waters were high and dangerous in order to carry a letter to its destination. They are exceedingly faithful in this business, having a superstitious dread of that mysterious power which makes *a paper talk without a mouth.*

The naked express-man having been hunted up, he was charged by Bidenger to proceed to Campo Seco without delay and to allow no one on the way to read the paper. The digger, as is usual with these native expresses, got him a small stick about two feet long, and splitting the end to the depth of an inch or two, stuck the letter into it, and holding it out in front of him, started off in a fast trot. One of Joaquín's party discovered him on the road, about three miles from Campo Seco, and wished to speak to him, but the Indian, remembering his charge, broke off at full speed, bearing the letter triumphantly before him. The robber fired two shots at the terrified native, which only accelerated his flight. Arriving at Campo Seco, he entered Beatty's office and handed him the following unique epistle:

FEBRUARY the 3 1853.

I hereby gave notice that there is a thief and robber In this Capulope by the name of wakeen he slep here last night and he Is xpected to sleap heare tonight thar is not men enough here that will Assist in taking him he has horses tide back hear in the hills and six more men
 i think it my duty to make it known.
     Alexander Bidenger and F. J. Mansfield.
    Rio Carrillo.   Bernardo Carasco.

The Justice, having deciphered the hieroglyphical characters of this letter as satisfactory as he could, sent a messenger to the keepers of the ferry at Winter's Bar to let no one cross during the night, believing that, from its proximity, that point would be selected by the robber for the passage of the river in case he was closely pursued, and hurried off the constable with a posse to rescue the six unfortunate men whom Joaquín had "tide" out in the hills. Arriving at Capulope in great heat, the constable ascertained that there were no six men tied out at all, but that the letter had designed to inform the Justice that Joaquín's party *numbered* six men.

"It's a pity," said Bidenger, "that a man of the Squire's larnin' can't read no better than that."

Nothing was seen of Joaquín in the neighborhood, though diligent search was made for him by the constable from the time he left Campo Seco until dark, but, at midnight, he rode up to the ferry at Winter's Bar and requested to be set over. The keepers informed him that they had orders from the civil authorities to let no one pass, not even the Governor of the State, whereupon the impatient outlaw made such unequivocal hostile demonstrations that the ferrymen were glad to set aside the civil authorities and, for the time being, to obey martial law.

A few days after this, riding along with Three-Fingered Jack and another member named Pedro, Joaquín met two Americans and a German coming on foot from the direction of Murphy's Diggings and bound for Australia as their final destination. They were laden with gold dust, which they intended to convert into bills of exchange at San Francisco, and committed the great imprudence to run at the approach of the bandits, who, having been hotly pursued a few hours before by a party of citizens, might have passed on without harming them. Seeing them take to flight, Joaquín said:

"Those fellows have money; we must kill them."

The poor, terrified fugitives each took a separate course, and it was not long before they miserably perished under the murderous pistols and knives of the bandits. Dragging them by the heels, the robbers, who had secured their heavy purses, threw them into a hole, which had been sunk by some prospectors and covered them partially with leaves and bushes.

Riding on a little farther upon a narrow pack-trail which wound along on the bank of a foaming stream that was almost hid in the deep gorge through which it ran, they suddenly come upon a Chinese camp, containing six Chinamen. Though each had a double-barreled shot-gun, they made no effort to defend themselves but begged for their lives. Joaquín was disposed to spare them, but, not wishing to leave his portrait impressed upon too many memories which might prove some day quite too tenacious for his good, he concluded to kill as well as rob them. Three-Fingered Jack, by a nod from Joaquín, stepped up to each one and led him out by his long tail of hair, repeating the ceremony until they all stood in a row before him. He then tied their tails securely together, searched their pockets, while Pedro ransacked their tents, and, drawing his highly-prized home-made knife, commenced, amid the howling and shrieks of the unfortunate Asiatics, splitting their skulls and severing their neck-veins. He was in his element, his eyes blazed, he shouted like a madman and leaped from one to the other, hewing and cutting, as if it afforded him the most exquisite satisfaction to revel in human agony.

"Come," said Joaquín, "that's enough, mount up, and let's be off."

Reaching the main road again in a few hours, they met the mail-rider between Jackson and Volcano, who, on perceiving them, laid whip to his very fleet animal and narrowly escaped. Three-Fingered Jack, on his fine black horse, could not in the whole race get nearer to him than fifty yards, and finally halted at that distance, and discharged three loads of his revolver at his slight figure, as he leaned forward with an apparent anxiety to go faster than his horse was carrying him.

"By God," said Garcia as he rode back to Joaquín, "I would like to have caught that fellow, if nothing more than to get his horse. He flung dirt into my face faster than I ever saw it fly from a horse's heels before."

While laughing over the very exhilarating race which they had just had, a man named H—— came in sight, and was within one hundred yards of the brigands before he perceived them. Three-Fingered Jack's appearance was enough for him without any further examination, and, wheeling his animal, a splendid mare, he proceeded to place as much ground as possible between himself and the dreaded party, which they, on the other hand, undertook to diminish. Neck and heel they had it for five miles, up the hills and down, Joaquín and Pedro a short distance behind and the "Knight of the Three Fingers" close on to the fugitive, who spared neither whip or spur, and, one time grasping at his bridle-rein, at another falling behind his horse's tail, and at another shooting at him with an unsuccessful aim. Straggling travelers on the road, Jew-peddlers, almond-eyed Chinamen, and deplorably ragged-looking Frenchmen, all, and everybody who happened to be on the road gave way to the frantic rider and his headlong pursuers, gazing at them with unmitigated astonishment and thanking their stars that *they* happened to be poor obscure footmen. H—— rode on, and on, and on, with unabated ardor on his own part, and no perceptible failure of vigor on the part of his horse until within sight of a thickly populated mining district, when, giving him a farewell shot which rang in unpleasant proximity to his ear, Three-Fingered Jack roared out to him:

"You *deserve* to escape, old fellow, success to you!" and galloped back to his comrades, who had halted a few minutes before. "There's another fine horse," said he to his leader, "that we've missed getting."

Numerous murders having been committed, and many parties having failed to capture the leading desperadoes, an excitement prevailed, almost too intense to be borne, in the whole county of Calaveras.

About the 19th of February, a large meeting was held at the town of Jackson, at which it was resolved that *everybody* should turn out in search of the villain Joaquín. A committee of six men were secretly sent at midnight to Mokelumne Hill to secure a concert of action there, upon whose arrival the citizens immediately assembled, and before morning, two companies were organized, horse and foot, and placed under the command of Charles A. Clark, Esq., then under-sheriff of the County. Thus was the whole country alive with armed parties, whose separate movements it would be impossible, without much unnecessary labor, to trace. Arrests were continually being made; popular tribunals established in the woods, Judge Lynch[38] installed upon the bench; criminals arraigned, tried, and executed upon the limb of a tree; pursuits, flights, skirmishes, and a topsy-turvy, hurly-burly mass of events that set narration at defiance. It remains only to give a few touches here and there that an idea may be gathered of the exciting picture which the state of things then presented.

The Jackson Company went down on the west side of the Mokelumne River, while Clark directed his companies to scour the woods and mountains in the direction of Campo Seco. From Campo Seco he went to Winter's

Bar, crossed the river, and rode up to Stone and Baker's Rancho, where he met the Jackson Company. Learning that Joaquín had lately been seen at Camp Opera, the united parties surrounded that place about daylight and huddled all the inhabitants, who were mostly Mexicans, together in a large tent, depriving them of their arms; and, upon questioning them, ascertained that a Mexican horseman had come into town the day before and inquired of some women, who were washing at the branch near by, if they had seen Joaquín—and that he paid one of them fifty cents for washing a handkerchief, deeply stained with blood. Upon closer questioning, it appeared that the Mexican spoken of was himself present in the tent, and he was, accordingly, led forth for the especial consideration of his case. Finding that the trial to which they subjected him was no farce and that they were actually going to hang him, he confessed that he was one of the brigands and submitted with great composure to be choked to death.

While their comrade was undergoing the penalty of death, Valenzuela and a few others, ignorant of the circumstance, were robbing a Dutchman only a few miles off from whom they took six hundred dollars in beautiful specimens, for which the poor fellow had honestly labored six months in the mines. He was fortunate, however, in meeting with Valenzuela instead of Three-Fingered Jack, for he escaped with his life after a long debate between the robbers as to the propriety of letting him live, in which the Dutchman afterwards acknowledged he was more interested than in any question he had ever heard discussed.

Capt. Ellas about this time heard of a suspicious fellow lurking around the little town of Camp of Los Muertos and mounting his horse, rode over to the tent in which he was harbored, and, with a pistol cocked in the villain's face, arrested him and took him to San Andreas. The people of that place appointed a committee to investigate the case and report their judgment as to what should be done in the premises. The Committee ascertained that he was wounded, a pistol-ball having pierced him in such a manner as to make four different holes, from a twisted posture, no doubt, which he had assumed, and, being able to elicit no satisfactory account as to how he had received the wound, they reported to the crowd that it was their opinion that it would not be amiss to hang him and to risk it anyhow, whether he was guilty or not. Finding that he had to go, he confessed that he was the man whom Ellas had shot on Chaparral Hill while he was endeavoring to catch his mare and that he was with Joaquín when the two Americans, Peter Woodbeck and another, were killed at the Phenix Quartz Mill. The time-honored custom of choking a man to death was soon put into practice, and the robber stood on nothing, kicking at empty space. Bah! it is a sight that I never like to see, although I have been civilized for a good many years.

On the 22d day of the month, one of the pursuing parties mentioned before came upon five Mexicans who were halted a few moments at a place called Forman's Camp and immediately fired upon them, wounding one of them in the hand. Outnumbered, the robbers, among whom was the chief himself, rode off at full speed. The Americans followed, and had not proceeded far when pistol-shots were heard in rapid succession at a Chinese camp at the foot of a hill, upon which they were riding. Hastening down to the spot, they found three Chinamen dead and five others writhing in their last agonies. The murderers were not more than ten minutes ahead. A dying Chinaman gasped out that they had been robbed of three thousand dollars. Exasperated beyond measure at such audacity, the party rode furiously on in pursuit, but their horses had not the mettle to compete with those of the brigands, and they were forced to give it up for that day. On the twenty-third they resumed the pursuit, passing no less than a dozen Chinese camps which had been recently plundered, and, towards evening, caught sight of the rascals on the summit of a hill, engaged at the moment in knocking down some Chinamen and robbing them. With a whoop of defiance, the daring chief led off his men before their faces with such speed that they could not hope, on their own common scrub horses, to overtake him.

The Chinese, beginning to believe that they were singled out for destruction, were seized with a general panic, and, by the fifth of March, might have been seen flocking from the mining districts in hundreds and thousands to the towns and cities. Mention the name of Joaquín to one of these Chinamen now, and his knees will quake like Belshazzar's.[39]

Having ravaged the county for several long and, to the people, distressing weeks, and having lost some of the bravest and most useful members of his band, and having aroused his enemies so that they met him on every trail and surprised him at almost every encampment; having, besides this, collected by his plunders a large amount of money, Joaquín concluded to abandon Calaveras and try his hand awhile upon the citizens of Mariposa. Of course that county suffered—but it will not be necessary to recount anything like the entire series of his fearful deeds in that devoted region, as it would only be a repetition of the bloody and harrowing scenes which have already sufficiently marked these pages. His guardian fiend seemed never to desert him, and he came forth from every emergency in triumph. The following incident is but one among many which shows the extraordinary success that attended him, and would almost lead us to adopt the old Cherokee superstition that there were some men who bear charmed lives and whom nothing can kill but a silver bullet.[40]

About the first of April, in the little town of Oanetas, or Little Ovens, an American named Prescott, a very bold and resolute man, was one night informed by a friendly Mexican, who was a miner in that district, that Joaquín and four or five of his men were at that moment sleeping in a house kept by a Mexican woman, on the edge of the town.

"If I point him out to you," said he, "be sure and kill him, for if you don't, my life is not worth three cents."

Prescott raised some fifteen men with secrecy and dispatch, and guided by the Mexican, gained the house without raising an alarm. Stationing his men around the house in every necessary direction, he and a few others cautiously entered. Candles were still burning, and everything was visible in the room.

"There they are," whispered the trembling Mexican, pointing to several separate heaps, rolled up in blankets, and slipping out as soon as he had spoken.

One of the party, holding a candle over Joaquín's face in his anxiety to see if there might not possibly be a mistake, startled the formidable chief from his slumber, who, with the rapid return of consciousness which belongs to men accustomed to danger, rose like lightening to his feet, cocking his pistol, as it were, in the very act of waking, and fired. The astounded candle-holder staggered back, severely wounded in the side. Prescott at this moment discharged both barrels of his shot-gun into Joaquín's breast, and was amazed to see him stand firm after a momentary stagger and return the fire. Prescott very near fell to the floor, a ball having passed clean through his chest. The other bandits in the meantime having sprung up, blew out the lights, and, firing their revolvers, immediately shifted their positions so that the Americans discharged their pistols into the space merely where their enemies had stood. Joaquín shot twice after the lights were extinguished, hitting a man each time, and, with his pistol clubbed, strode resolutely for the door. Here he met an American, over whose head he shattered his pistol, very nearly killing him on the spot. It happened that, at the same time the bandits made their egress, a few Americans were also coming out, and, before the two parties could be fairly separated so as to render it safe to fire, the bold robbers had made their escape.

It is significant to add that in a few days after this occurrence, the Mexican informer was found hanging to a tree near the highway, his dead body bearing the marks of a recent terrible scourging. Joaquín was badly wounded by the discharge of Prescott's double-barreled shot-gun, and Three-Fingered Jack, who was now continually with him, was engaged (as he laughingly remarked to an acquaintance afterwards) for three weeks, off and on, in picking out buck-shot from his breast.

"How it come not to kill him," said he, "the devil only knows. I'm certain it would have done the job for me."

But subsequent events will show that Three-Fingered Jack was himself equally hard to kill. Prescott lay for a long time in a doubtful state, and Joaquín sent spies daily, from his own sick-bed in the woods, to see if there was any prospect of his dying. Much to his disappointment, Prescott recovered, and surely, after all he had suffered, he is entitled to live a long time.

Valenzuela was, at this time, in the county of Yuba, in obedience to the orders of his leader who told him to do his best in the space of two weeks and then to meet him at the Arroyo Cantoova rendezvous.

A description of one or two scenes which happened on Bear River, about twenty miles from the city of Marysville, will serve to give an idea of what he was about. This stream heads in the Sierra Nevada foot-hills, and, crossing a broad plain, empties into Feather River near the town of

Nicolaus. It waters a fine agricultural and grazing region, and houses in the spring of 1853, as now, were scattered at intervals of four, five, and six miles along its banks. In one of these houses lived an old wicow woman, with her son and daughter. These three, seated in their door on a pleasant evening, were surprised, as they lived off from the public road, to see four huge fellows ride up, splendidly dressed, and armed to the teeth. One of them had four revolvers and a bowie-knife. Dismounting, they requested supper. It was soon got in readiness by the brisk young lady—and she is as fresh and rosy a creature as ever one had the happiness to see—and the travelers partook of it most freely; the fellow with the four revolvers, who, notwithstanding his fierce look, was quite gentlemanly in his manners, conversing with her agreeably as she politely waited upon them. The old woman looked rather suspiciously at the well-dressed eaters from under her spectacles but said nothing. As soon as they had finished, Valenzuela, for it was that worthy and none other, stepped up to where the young man was sitting and, cocking a pistol between his eyes, asked him if he had any objection to having the house robbed—if so, to name it. The old woman here screamed out:

"Oh, Lord! I knowed it—I seed the cloven-foot[41] a'stickin out all the time," and continued to cry out with such vehemence that they were forced to put a gag in her mouth. The young lady saved them the trouble of using that precaution in her case by fainting.

The young man, not relishing a cocked pistol in his face with a man carelessly fingering the trigger, very readily gave his consent to have the house searched. Every drawer was ransacked and every trunk burst open, and, having obtained a few hundred dollars, the robbers left.

At a late hour in the night, another house was burst open, and the terrified inmates were dragged out of their beds, and securely bound hand and foot, besides being gagged, before they awoke sufficiently to know whether it was a dream or a reality. There was only one man at the house, the rest were women and children. All the money and jewelry was taken that could be found, and among other things, a gold watch, the chain of which Valenzuela very coolly put over his neck.

"Go to that old woman and take the gag out of her mouth," said he to one of his men, "she looks as if she were choking herself to death in the effort to say something."

As soon as the gag was removed, she begged Valenzuela, with many tears, to give her back the watch, as it was a present from a dear friend who was dead, and contained a precious lock of hair.

"Certainly," said the robber, "if that's the case, I don't want it," and handed it to her.

Strange as it may seem at the first glance, the aged widow felt a sentiment of gratitude towards the robber, who, steeped in villainy as he was, had soul enough to answer an appeal of this kind. The unfortunate family were found the next morning by their neighbors, still lying upon the floor, bound hand and foot.

Such terror possessed that neighborhood for some time afterwards that a traveler, no matter how peaceable his intentions, could no more get a chance to stay all night on that part of Bear River than he could fly. A young fellow from the mountains on his way down the valley, happening to be belated in that vicinity, called one night at every house in every direction, and was refused admittance or hospitality, with an obstinacy which astonished him. The doors were barred on his approach as if he had been a bearer of pestilence, and, to his loud haloos and earnest solicitations for shelter from the night air, he received the response that they had "no accommodation for travelers," and he began to believe that indeed they *did* have but little accommodation, sure enough! It was drizzling rain, the hour was waxing late, it was dark, and there were many deep and miry sloughs, which it was dangerous to pass unless in broad daylight. Directed, at each refusal of "accommodation," to go to another house "just across the slough," or "jist beyant that pint," the poor fellow wandered around nearly all night, narrowly escaping being drowned a dozen times; finally, towards morning, leaving his horse tied on the bank of a slough and crossing to the other side in a canoe, he succeeded, after fighting a pitched battle with a gang of fierce dogs, in reaching an old shanty in a barley field, whose occupant, a bachelor, consented, to his great surprise, to let him stay. It seems that the young fellow was dark-skinned and, unfortunately, not a very amiable-looking fellow at the best, and he was, accordingly, taken for Joaquín or some one of his band traveling around as a spy.

So burdensome were the tributes levied upon the citizens of the whole State by the robbers, and so ceaselessly did they commit their depredations that it became a fit subject for legislative action. A petition, numerously signed, was presented to the Legislature,[42] praying that body to authorize Captain Harry Love to organize a company of Mounted Rangers in order to capture, drive out of the country, or exterminate the desperate bands of highwaymen, who placed in continual jeopardy both life and property. A bill to this effect was passed and signed by the Governor on the 17th of May, 1853, and a company was organized by Harry Love on the 28th of the same month. The pay was set down at one hundred and fifty dollars a month per man, and the legal existence of the company limited to three months, while the number of men was not to exceed twenty. Notwithstanding the small amount of wages allowed, each member was required to furnish his own horse, provisions, and equipments at his individual expense. Without hesitation, nay, with alacrity, for it was in consonance with his daring spirit, Love immediately took the command of twenty choice men, selected for their well-known courage, and led them forth to meet as formidable a man as ever figured in the arena of crime. This brave, but small, party of Mounted Rangers were looked upon by the anxious eyes of the community, from whose midst they started, as almost certainly destined to destruction. But they forgot that a leader was now in the field and armed with the authority of the State whose experience was a part of the stormiest histories of the frontier settlements, the civil commotions of Texas, and the Mexican war, whose soul was as rugged and severe as the discipline through which it had passed, whose brain was as strong and clear in the midst of dangers as that of the daring robber against whom he was sent, and who possessed a glance as quick and a hand as sudden in the execution of a deadly purpose.

With untiring energy and the most stealthy movements, Capt. Love set himself to work to obtain a full knowledge of the haunts of the bandit-chief, the latest traces of his steps, and all that was necessary to enable him to fall upon him at the best possible time and place. While on this look-out for him, Joaquín was busy in making his preparations for the grand finale of his career in California. After robbing extensively on the Little Mariposa and the Merced River, he proceeded to the rancho of Joaquín Guerra, near to San José, killing on his way a Frenchman who kept the well-known Tivola Gardens,[43] and there stopped for a few weeks, lying concealed. The *Major Domo*[44] of this rancho, Francisco Sicarro, was secretly connected with his band, and this accounts for his staying there. In the meantime, he had dispatched Luis Vulvia to the Arroyo Cantoova with orders to remove the women to a place of safety in the province of Sonora; to send Valenzuela, as soon as he should arrive at the rendezvous, to the same State with remittances of money and with instructions to arm and equip his followers and adherents there, who stood in waiting; and to proceed himself to the different harboring-ranchos in California and collected at the Arroyo Cantoova all the horses which had been left upon them from time to time. It was his own intention to go to the rendezvous in a short time and wait for the arrival of his forces. The extreme caution with which this wily leader was bringing his plans to a focus is aptly exhibited in the following comparatively little incident.

Feeling, one evening, somewhat inclined for a dram and unwilling to show his own person, he sent from Guerra's Rancho an Indian to bring him a bottle of liquor from San José. After the Digger had started, he became a little uneasy, lest the fellow should betray him, and, mounting his horse, overtook him on the road, near to Cayote Creek, and killed him.

On the first day of July, seventy of his followers had arrived at the Arroyo Cantoova with fifteen hundred horses, and, in another part of the valley, Joaquín himself, with Reis, Three-Fingered Jack, and a few other men, was waiting for the final arrival of all his forces from Sonora and other quarters. His correspondence was large with many wealthy and influential Mexicans residing in the State of California, and he had received assurances of their earnest co-operation in the movement which he contemplated. A shell was about to burst which was little dreamed of by the mass of the people, who merely looked upon Joaquín as a petty leader of a band of cut-throats!

On the fifth of July, Capt. Love, who had been secretly tracing the bandit in his movements, left, with his company, the town of San José and camped near San Juan for four or five days, scouring the mountains in that vicinity. From San Juan, he started in the night on the coast route in the direction of Los Angeles and tarried a night or two on the Salinas Plains. Thence he went across the San Bonita Valley, camping just before daylight, without being discovered by any one, in a small valley in the coast range, near to Quien Sabe Rancho. Leaving this place after a short survey of the neighborhood, he proceeded to the Eagle's Pass and there came upon a party of Mexicans who were going, or said so at least, into the Tulares to capture the wild mustangs which fed there in great numbers. From this point, the Rangers divided, a portion going to the Chico Panoche Pass and the others taking a course through the mountains. They found trails which led both divisions to the same point, that is, to the Bayou Seetas, or Little Prairie. Before reaching this point, Love stopped a few Mexicans, who were evidently carrying forward the news of his advance into that wild and suspicious region. Separating again, the company again met at the Grande Panoche Pass, from which they went on in a body to the Arroyo Cantoova. Here they found the seventy or eighty men of Joaquín's band spoken of above, with the fifteen hundred stolen horses. These men, it would be fair to infer, could have annihilated the small party of twenty men opposed to them had they seen fit, and it was a wise act in Capt. Love to deceive them as he did by informing them that he was executing a commission, on the part of the State, to obtain a list of all the names of those who were engaged in mustang-hunting, in order that a tax might be collected from them for the privilege, in accordance with a late act of the Legislature. With this explanation, and going through the farce of taking down a list of their names, which were no doubt fictitious, every one of them, he started on in the direction of San Juan but turned about and stopped seven or eight miles off at the head of the Arroyo, in order to watch their movements. It was now the 24th of the month, on the morning of which day he went back to their encampment and found it wholly deserted, not a man or a horse left. Fully convinced from this sudden abandonment of the place that they were nothing less than a portion of Joaquín's band, he resolved to follow their trail. On the 25th, which was Sunday, at 3 o'clock in the morning, he reached the Tulare Plains, where he found they had parted their company—some going south towards the Tejon Pass and others north towards the San Joaquin River. Detailing a portion of the Rangers to proceed to Mariposa County with some stolen horses which had been recovered on the way, the Captain, with the remainder of his party, numbering only eight men, dauntlessly pursued the southern trail which led in the more proper direction for finding Joaquín. Just at daylight, he saw a smoke rising from the plains on his left, and, wishing to allow no circumstance, however trivial, to pass unnoticed at a time so much requiring his utmost vigilance, he turned from the trail and rode out towards it. He saw nothing more than some loose horses until within six hundred yards of the spot from which the smoke proceeded, when, rising a mound, he discovered, in a little hollow, seven men scattered around a small fire, one of whom was a few steps off, washing a fine-looking bay horse, out of a pan. Their sentinel, who had just been cooking, at this moment caught sight of the approaching party and gave the alarm to his comrades, who all rushed forth in the direction of their horses, except the man who already held his by the lariat at camp. Dashing up in hot haste, the Rangers succeeded in stopping every man before he got to his animal. The Captain, riding up to the individual who stood holding the horse, questioned him as to the course upon which he and the others were traveling. He answered that they were going to Los Angeles. Giving the nod to two of his young men, Henderson and White, they stood watching this individual while the Captain rode towards others of the suspicious-looking party, who, I have omitted to say, were all Mexicans, superbly dressed, each wearing over their finery a costly broadcloth cloak. Addressing one of these others in relation to their destination, he replied in direct contradiction to what the first had just said, who, flushing up with an angered look, exclaimed:

"No! we're going to Los Angeles"; and, turning to Love, said: "Sir, if you have any questions to ask, address yourself to me. I am the leader of this company."

Love answered "that he would address himself to whom he pleased, without consulting him."

The leader, as he called himself, then advanced a few steps towards the saddles and blankets, which lay around the fire, when Love told him to stop. He walked on without heeding the command when the Captain drew his six-shooter and told him if he did not stop in an instant, he would blow his brains out. With a proud toss of his head and grating his teeth together in rage, he stepped back and laid his hand again upon his horse's mane, which had stood quietly during the moment he was away. This individual was Joaquín Murieta, though Love was ignorant of the fact. He was armed only with a bowie-knife and was advancing towards his saddle to get his pistols when Love drew his revolver on him and made him stop. A short distance off stood Three-Fingered Jack, fully armed, and anxtiously watching every motion of his chief. Separated by the Rangers, surprised, and unable to act in concert; on foot and unable to get to their horses were scattered, here and there, others of the party. The danger to Joaquín was great and imminent, yet no sign of fear played upon his countenance. He held his head firmly and looked around him with a cool and unflinching glance, as if he calmly studied the desperate chances of the time. He patted, from time to time, his horse upon the neck, and the fiery steed raised his graceful head, pricked up his sharply-pointed ears, and stood, with flashing eyes, as if ready to spring at a moment's warning. Lieut. Byrnes, who had known the young robber when he was an honest man a few years before soon rode into camp, having fallen behind by order of the Captain, and immediately on his approach, Joaquín, who knew him at the first sight, called out to his followers to make their escape, every man for himself. Three-Fingered Jack bounded off like a mighty stag of the forest. He was shot at by several of the Rangers, and, attention being momentarily called away from Joaquín, he mounted his fine, bay horse, already eager to run, and rode off without saddle or bridle at the speed of the wind. A dozen balls from the Colt's repeaters whizzed by him without effect. Rushing along a rough and rocky ravine with that recklessness that belongs to a bold rider and a powerful, high-spirited animal, he leaped from a precipice, ten or twelve feet high, and was thrown violently from his horse, which turned a half-somerset as he touched the ground and fell on his back with his heels in a few inches of his master's head. Horse and rider recovering themselves in a moment, Joaquín again mounted with the quickness of lightning, and was again on the wing. One of his pursuers, named Henderson, fearlessly leapt after him, while others, who were not so close behind, galloped around to head him at a certain favorable point. Henderson and horse went through the same motions of lofty tumbling, as in the example which had preceded him. He was not mounted so soon but that Joaquín was some distance ahead before he was fairly ready to renew the chase. The bold chieftain was fast escaping danger on his swift and beautiful steed, and a few more vigorous bounds would carry him beyond the reach of gun-shot, when one of the pursuing party, finding that they could not hit the rider, levelled his rifle at the horse and sent a ball obliquely into his side. The noble animal sunk a moment but rose again, still vigorous, though bleeding, and was hearing his master as if he knew that his life depended upon *him*, clearly out of all reach of a bullet or any fear of a capture, when alas! for the too exulting hopes of the youthful chieftain, the poor beast, with a sudden gush of blood from his mouth and nostrils, fell dead beneath him. A fortunate shot, whoever aimed that rifle! Joaquín, now far ahead of his pursuers, ran on, on foot. They outran him upon their horses, and, coming again in pistol-shot, discharged several balls into his body. When the third ball struck him, he turned around, facing them, and said:

"Don't shoot any more—the work is done."

He stood still a few moments, turning pale as his life-blood ebbed away, and, sinking slowly to the ground upon his right arm, surrendered to death.

While their beloved leader was proudly submitting to the inexorable Fate which fell upon him, if we may call it Fate when it was born from his own extreme carelessness in separating himself from the main body of his men and in a habitual feeling of too much security at his rendez-vous, his followers were struggling for their lives against fearful odds in all directions over the plains. Three-Fingered Jack, pursued by Love himself and one or two others, ran five miles before he fell, pierced with nine balls. He leaped over the ground like a wild beast of the chase and frequently gained a considerable distance on his pursuers, whose horses would sometimes tumble in the gopher holes and soft soil of the plain and throw their riders headlong in the dirt. When overtaken, he would wheel with glaring eyes, and, with a whoop of defiance, discharge his six-shooter. Though a good shot, out of five trials he missed every time. Circumstances were against him, but he was determined never to be taken alive, and to no proposal to surrender would he listen a moment, but ran on as long as his strength would sustain him, and fought till he fell, dying with his hand on his pistol, which he had emptied of every load but one. He was, at last, shot through the head by Capt. Love, who had wounded him twice before in the long chase. Three-Fingered Jack, anomalous as it may seem to be since he was the very incarnation of cruelty, was, at the same time, as brave a man as this world ever produced, and so died as those who killed him will testify.

Shortly after the chase of Joaquín and Three-Fingered Jack commenced, three of the band, not before discovered, galloped out into the plain from a point a little below Joaquín's camp-fire where they had probably made a small, separate encampment the night before, and dismounted in full view of several of the Rangers, who approached them on three sides. They stood still until within reach of pistol-shot, when they suddenly sprang into their saddles, and, firing their revolvers at the approaching Rangers, rode off. The Rangers returned the fire with effect, wounding two of the men and one of the horses. Their animals being remarkably swift, they distanced their pursuers and reached the foot of the mountains without further injury. But just at this point, one of the wounded men grew so faint that he fell back in the flight, and, a comrade falling back also to assist him, thus gave the Rangers an opportunity to come within gunshot. As he galloped off with his wounded companion to rejoin his brothers ahead, a skillful marksman levelled a rifle at his retreating figure and sent a ball into his back that made him reel upon his horse, and thus added one more to the wounded list, which now comprised the whole party. They succeeded in escaping, but one of them fell from his horse during the following night and died in a solitary place among the mountains.

The pursuit being ended on all parts of the field, the Rangers returned to the point from which they had started. As yet, all were ignorant of the true character of the party which they had attacked. Byrnes did not happen to be looking at Joaquín when he first rode into camp, and consequently had not recognized him at all, not being with the individuals who succeeded in killing him. When they all got together, it was ascertained that four Mexicans had been killed and two others taken prisoners. Going up to the dead bodies, one was immediately recognized by Byrnes as that of Joaquín Murieta and another, by some one else, as that of Three-Fingered Jack.

It was important to prove, to the satisfaction of the public, that the famous and bloody bandit was actually killed, else the fact would be eternally doubted, and many unworthy suspicions would attach to Capt. Love. He, accordingly, acted as he would not otherwise have done; and I must shock the nerves of the fastidious, much against my will, by stating that he caused the head of the renowned Murieta to be cut off and to be hurried away with the utmost expedition to the nearest place, one hundred and fifty miles, at which any alcohol could be obtained in which to preserve it. Three-Fingered Jack's head was also cut off, but being shot through, soon became offensive, and was throw away. His hand, however, was preserved—that terrible, three-fingered hand—which had dyed itself in many a quivering heart—had torn with its ruthless *talons* the throats of many an agonized victim, and had shadowed itself forth upon the horrified imaginations of thousands who only knew that it existed. The head, which for a long time retained a very natural appearance, was carried for exhibition over a large portion of the State and thoroughly identified in every quarter where its owner was known. The hand was also exhibited in a glass case, not to prove its identity (though even that was done) but to give the public the actual sight of an object which had flung a strange, haunting dread over the mind, as if it had been a conscious, voluntary agent of evil. Many superstitious persons, ignorant of the phenomenon which death presents in the growth of the hair and nails, were seized with a kind of terror to observe that the moustache of the fearful robber had grown longer since his head was cut off and that the nails of Three-Fingered Jack's hand had lengthened almost an inch.

The bloody encounter being over, Love gathered up the spoils, which consisted of seven fine animals (afterwards restored to their owners), six elegant Mexican saddles and bridles, six Colt's revolvers, a brace of holster pistols, and five or six pairs of spurs. Three splendid horses were killed under their riders in the chase. Five or six fine broadcloth cloaks were found at the camp. Money, there was none; one of the prisoners, however, declared that Three-Fingered Jack, during the chase, threw away a very large purse of gold, which was encumbering him in his flight; and it is probable that others did the same.

Upon the return of the Rangers from this expedition, one of the prisoners, after vainly endeavoring to persuade his companion to follow his example, suddenly broke loose from his captors, and, plunging into a deep slough near by, bravely drowned himself. The other was taken to Mariposa County Jail, and there confined until the company were ready to disband, when he was transferred to Martinez. While there, he made a confession, implicating a large number of his countrymen in the villainies which had been perpetrated, and was prepared to make still more important disclosures—perhaps with the view of making the value of his information weigh against his execution—when he was forestalled in a mysterious manner. The jail was broken open one night at the dead hours and the prisoner taken out by an armed mob and hung. The Americans knew nothing of the hanging, so that the most rational conjecture is that he was put out of the way by Mexicans to prevent the damning revelations which he would certainly have made.

After a thorough identification of the head of Joaquín, the Governor of the State, Colonel John Bigler, caused to be paid to Captain Love the sum of one thousand dollars, which, in his official capacity, he had offered for the capture of the bandit, dead or alive. And subsequently, on the fifteenth day of May, 1854, the Legislature of California, considering that his truly valuable services in ridding the country of so great a terror—were not sufficiently rewarded, passed an act granting him an additional sum of five thousand dollars.

The story is told. Briefly and without ornament, the life and character of Joaquín Murieta have been sketched. His career was short, for he died in his twenty-second year; but, in the few years which were allowed him, he displayed qualities of mind and heart which marked him as an extraordinary man, and leaving his name impressed upon the early history of this State. He also leaves behind him the important lesson that there is nothing so dangerous in its consequences as *injustice to individuals*—whether it arise from prejudice of color or from any other source; that a wrong done to one man is a wrong to society and to the world.

It is only necessary to add that after the death of its chief, the mighty organization which he had established was broken up. It exists now only in scattered fragments over California and Mexico. Its subordinate chiefs, among whom is the now living Joaquín Valenzuela—lacking the brilliancy and unconquerable will of their leader—will never be able to revive it in its full force; and, although all the elements are still in active existence, they will make themselves felt in nothing more, it is probable, than petty out-breaks, here and there, and depredations of such a character as can easily be checked by the vigilance of the laws.

Of Rosita, the beautiful and well-beloved of Joaquín, nothing further is known than that she remains in the Province of Sonora, silently and sadly working out the slow task of a life forever blighted to her, under the roof of her aged parents. Alas, how happy might she not have been, had man never learned to wrong his fellow-man!

Death of Joaquín

Appendix

Unsigned, *The Life of Joaquin Murieta the Brigand Chief of California; Being A Complete History of His Life, from the Age of Sixteen to the Time of his Capture and Death at the Hands of Capt. Harry Love, in the Year 1853.* San Francisco: Published at Office of the "California Police Gazette," 1859. Pgs. 6–7, 15–16, 16–17, 21, 70–71.

This unsigned, plagiarized version of Ridge's novel circulated much more widely than the original. Serialized in the California Police Gazette, *a weekly publication featuring stories of sensational crimes,* The Life of Joaquin Murieta the Brigand Chief of California *became the basis of numerous translations and reworkings of the story, including Ireneo Paz's* Vida y aventuras del más célebre bandido sonorense, Joaquín Murrieta *(1904).*

The following passage, which recounts Murieta's first revenge killing, adds a long, stylized monologue in which Murieta justifies his crime by recalling the murder of his beloved (named Carmela, not Rosita, in this version).

"What—what means this?" gasped the victim as he sank to the ground, "why do you murder me? oh! mercy—spare my life."

"You showed no mercy to me," replied Joaquin, "when you assisted in tying and lashing me in the presence of a multitude of people. When, in the proud consciousness of your strength, and supported by the brute force of some of your own countrymen, you seized upon an innocent man—a *man*—with heart and soul, and all the noble attributes received from his Maker—a man possessed of more truth and honor than could have been found among those who helped to torture him; when you seized him and bound him, and scored his back with the ignominious lash, you did not then think of *mercy*. When your countrymen hung my brother by the neck like a dog, was there any mercy shown him? When they cruelly murdered my heart's dearest treasure, in my own presence and almost before my eyes; and when she must, with her silvery voice, have faintly appealed for mercy, was that appeal heeded by the inhuman wretches? Ah! my brain is on fire!" he added, pressing his left hand to his forehead, while with the other he inflicted another wound.

"Murder!" muttered the doomed man, raising himself upon his elbow and staring with wild, glassy eyes upon the savage features of the desperado, "Oh! mercy—mer—," but the steel had now entered his heart and he fell back a corpse.

Again and again was the knife plunged into the body, until the latter was almost hacked to pieces, for the demon of revenge possessed the soul of Joaquin and urged him to excess.

"Now, thus have I commenced this work of death!" he hissed through his closed teeth, as he drew himself up to his full height and gazed upon the blue expanse above him, while from the weapon in his outstretched hand still dripped the crimson fluid, "thus have I lain one of my base oppressors at my feet, and having so initiated my hand and heart, shall know no rest nor peace until every one of them is blotted from the earth; and oh! dearest Carmela, you whose spirit I believe is even now hovering over me, you too shall be terribly avenged; my arm is nerved for the work of destruction, and the life-blood of the Americans shall flow as freely as the mountain stream."

The following passage substitutes Guerro's story about fighting alongside the Mexican guerrilla Padre Jurata for Valenzuela's story from Ridge's novel (see pages 63–65). Whereas Valenzuela recounts a daring escape from an ambush by American soldiers, the California Police Gazette *depicts Jurata's men as the aggressors who ambush and kill a group of American soldiers so impetuously that Jurata accidentally decapitates one of his own followers.*

"Well, comrades," resumed Guerro, "as you seem to be very anxious to know as much as possible about the old priest, I'll relate the adventure for the benefit of those among us who have not had the pleasure of serving under him. Well, you see, one night the Padre and myself and twenty-five others were jogging along on our mustangs at an easy trot, and had just entered a thick chaparral in order to make a short cut to a watering-place, when Jurata observed a thin, light colored smoke curling up into the air, at about a quarter of a mile ahead of us. 'Halt and dismount!' he suddenly exclaimed, 'remove your spurs, tie your horses, and follow me in silence,' at the same moment sliding from his own saddle, he unbuckled his jingling silver heel-trappings, and with an impatient wave of his hand, darted through the thicket. With quick and noiseless step we bounded after our leader, our hearts beating with anxious desire for blood and booty, and our hands ready to execute any and every order of the fearless padre. On we went, through tangled brush, drawing nearer and nearer to the slowly rising column of smoke, till at length we reached the bank of a deep and gloomy looking gulch, through which a noisy stream was leaping and sparkling in the moonlight. On looking down, Santa Maria! what a scene met our delighted vision. Around the smouldering embers of a few half-burned logs, lay a score of men, covered with the heavy, coarse blue overcoats of the American army. Their muskets were stacked at a short distance from them, and all unconscious of danger, they were resting from the fatigue, perhaps, of a long and toilsome march. Like serpents we glided down, and at a signal from Jurata, sprang upon them with our knives. Caramba! how they did squirm, and kick, and yell! 'Finish them speedily!' shouted the padre, while he himself humped from one to another, sheathing his dripping blade in the bodies of the dead as well as the living, and in a perfect frenzy of excitement severing the neck-joints and casting the gaping heads into the rushing water. It was a glorious affair, *paysanos,* and was only marred by a single unfortunate incident. One of our men, a brave fellow who possessed great influence in the band, had thoughtlessly enwrapped himself in one of the dead men's coats, and Jurata, mistaking him for an American, with a sudden and violent plunge of his huge bowie-knife, stretched him lifeless at his feet. The mistake was only discovered when the padre, holding the ghastly head for an instant in the dim rays of the moon, previous to hurling it into the stream, saw the large, black, glassy eyes of Francisco, gazing full upon him. 'Holy Virgin!' he shouted, 'what have I done!' and jumping back to the body, he tore open the coat and beheld the well known form of one of his bravest followers. 'Oh, fool! fool!' he added, 'you have well deserved your fate for encasing yourself in that hated garment, and were it possible, I would punish you with a thousand deaths;' and after burying his bloody knife several times in the inanimate breast of Francisco, he led the way back to where the animals were picketed, and solemnly resumed the journey."

"A lively story," said Joaquin, "and if the padre, Heaven rest his soul! were alive now, I would send for him, and resign to him the command of my brave little army."

In the following passage and others, the California Police Gazette *exaggerates the anti-Chinese violence depicted in Ridge's novel. Here, Three-Fingered Jack orchestrates the torture and killing of Chinese miners as an "entertainment" for Murieta's followers (and implicitly for readers as well). And in this version, Murieta and his men are all complicit in Three-Fingered Jack's brutal killings, and his lover is named Clarina, not Rosita.*

Three-Fingered Jack at this moment reappeared, driving before him no less than eight terrified Celestials, who on finding themselves in the presence of so many armed men, fell upon their knees, and in a by no means euphonious tongue, pleaded for mercy. Their lugubrious supplications, rolling eyes, and general ridiculous appearance, only excited the merriment of the band, who made the woods echo and re-echo with long and loud peals of laughter. The poor Chinamen were then ordered by the captor, by words and signs, to change their position and seat themselves against a rocky ledge, a few feet from the fire. The order was obeyed with considerable alacrity, and Three-Fingered Jack, after brandishing his knife over their heads, and telling them "if they moved he would cut their hearts out," again commenced upon the sardines and crackers with a good appetite.

"Ah!—Jack, *mi amigo*," said Joaquin, "how came this fresh blood upon the blade of your knife?"

"Well, I was obliged to kill one of the rascals, before I could bring the others to terms; but as soon as they saw the fellow laid out, one of them with a little more instinct than the rest, took the lead, and like sheep, the balance followed, and so I drove them up."

"And now that they are here, what do you intend to do with them?" inquired Antonio.

"Why, *kill* them like sheep, of course."

"Better do it at once then," suggested Feliz, "for they are half frightened to death already."

"Oh, they'll keep," replied Jack, glaring ferociously at his prisoners, "I brought them for the amusement of the company, but must finish my supper before I begin the entertainment. I have adopted the American maxim of '*business before pleasure.*'"

After a lapse of fifteen minutes, which had been passed by Jack in eating and by the other bandits in smoking, the former jumped towards the Chinamen, and tying seven of them together by their cues [*sic*], brought the eighth close to the fire, some of the band having moved a little aside to make room.

"Stop! stop! Jack," said Guerro, "you are not going to *burn* him—we can't stand *that* on a *sardine* stomach!"

"Oh, no, I've only brought him up close, so that you can the better witness the performance;" and drawing his knife, he drove it with powerful force into the heart of the trembling Celestial; then instantly withdrawing the weapon, he supported the victim with both hands, while a stream of blood spurted out and partly extinguished the fire.

"Carrajo!" exclaimed one of the men, "you are spattering me all over."

"And putting out the fire too;" said another.

"Come, Jack, let us have no more of this," rejoined Joaquin, impatiently, "such cruelty is disgusting and sickening; dispatch them at once, where they are, and have done with it."

"Oh, very well; as you like, Capitan; I thought the company wanted some amusement; but I shall now have all the pleasure to myself;" and after dragging away the corpse and throwing it carelessly down, Garcia leaped upon the other captives, and despite their screams, entreaties, and struggles, proceeded leisurely to cut their throats one after the other.

Previous to the killing of the first, the three females had drawn their serapes over their heads, unwilling to witness the fiendish act, and trembling with affright at the idea of being made accessory to the murder of so many helpless beings. Clarina, who was seated by the side of the bandit chief, had heard his order to dispatch the prisoners and with a true feeling of compassion, attempted to save the remainder from their horrid fate. Without uncovering her face she leaned her head upon her lover's shoulder and exclaimed in a voice tremulous with emotion:

"Ah, Joaquin, why do you not prevent this terrible slaughter—this unnecessary destruction of human life. Hear those despairing cries! those shrieks for mercy! you have power—will you not stay the murderer's hand?"

"Alas! dearest, I cannot; Garcia is impetuous and cruel, and it was only to gratify his unquenchable thirst for blood that he joined the band; but he is brave even to recklessness, and I can ill afford to lose him."

"Then their doom is sealed," murmured Clarina.

"It is, and I pity them from my very heart. Listen! there are now but *two* voices pleading, and now—*only one,* and *that* is suddenly stifled. The work is done, and they no longer suffer."

"Ha! Murieta," exclaimed Three-Fingered Jack, as he reseated himself in front of the fire, "by all the saints! This has been a glorious night for me; what a delightful time I have had with those wretches, and how little they resisted. San Miguel! what a luxurious feast of blood!"

This passage, in which Three-Fingered Jack helps accomplish Murieta's revenge for the rape and murder of Carmela, reiterates Murieta's reliance on his associate's bloodthirsty nature.

The travelers had passed on a few yards, and were walking along at an easy gait, with no apprehension of danger, when the simultaneous report of four pistols rang upon the air, and three of the doomed men fell apparently in the agonies of death. The fourth being only slightly wounded, turned to look upon the assailants.

"Ha! Americano! do you know *me*? I am Joaquin!" cried the bandit chief, and firing three shots in quick succession, sent forth a long, loud whoop of joyful satisfaction as he saw the man sink lifeless by the side of his companions.

"Now! Jack," he continued, pointing to the bodies, "*this* time I not only give you *permission*, but I *command* you, to exercise your natural propensity. Some of them may be still alive; at any rate, their blood is not yet cold."

Three-Fingered Jack had started at the first word of his leader, and was already half-way across, wading in the muddy stream to his arm pits. In another minute, he clambered up to the opposite bank and commenced his horrid work. With a shout of exultation he discovered that two of the men were not mortally wounded, but still so disabled as to make escape impossible; and heedless of their cries and struggles, the demon slowly disemboweled them, and finished the sickening scene by cutting out their hearts.

When Three-Fingered Jack returned to the tent, he inquired the cause of the chief's particular hatred towards those men.

"Jack," replied Joaquin, "three of them were of the party who murdered my Carmela and drove me from my home in the mines. Who the other man was I know not; but he deserved his fate for being found in such company."

> *The final pages of the* California Police Gazette *edition reprint a poster and two affidavits connected with the exhibition of Murieta's head. While this apparently affirms the finality of Murieta's alleged death, the novel goes on to recount further raids by Murieta's men and the mysterious deaths of the men who bought and sold his head at auction.*

The head was then placed on exhibition, in order to give the public an opportunity to see and judge for themselves; and the following advertisement informed them where the horrid trophy could be found.

JOAQUIN'S HEAD
IS TO BE SEEN
AT KING'S!
Corner Halleck and Sansome streets,
opposite the American Theatre.
Admission.. . . .. One Dollar

The following were among the many affidavits, certificates, etc., proving the identity of the head:

STATE OF CALIFORNIA, } SS.
County of San Francisco.

Ignacio Lisarrago, of Sonora, being duly sworn, says: That he has seen the alleged head of Joaquin, now in the possession of Messrs. Nuttall and Black, two of Capt. Love's Rangers, on exhibition at the saloon of John King, Sansome street. That deponent was well acquainted with

Joaquin Murieta, and that the head exhibited as above, is and was the veritable head of Joaquin Murieta, the celebrated bandit.

(Signed,)   IGNACIO LISARRAGO.

Sworn to before me, this 17th day of August, A. D. 1853.

CHARLES D. CARTER,
Notary Public.

STATE OF CALIFORNIA,   } SS.
County of San Joaquin.

On this, the 11th day of August, 1853, personally came before me, A. C. Baine, a Justice of the Peace for said county, the Rev. Father Dominie Blaive, who makes oath, in due form of law, that he was acquainted with the notorious robber, Joaquin; that he has just examined the captive's head, now in the possession of Capt. Conner, of Harry Love's Rangers, and that he verily believes the said head to be that of the individual Joaquin Murieta, so known by him two years ago, as before stated.

D. BLAIVE.

Sworn to and subscribed before me, the day aforesaid.   A. C. Baine, J. P.

The head, which for a long time retained a very natural appearance, was identified in every part of the State, wherever it was exhibited. The hand of Three-Fingered Jack was shown in another glass case at the same time, and some superstitious persons were not a little terrified on observing that the nails of the hand had grown nearly an inch since it was cut off.

After a thorough identification, the Governor of the State, Col. John Bigler, caused to be paid to Capt. Love the sum of one thousand dollars, which in his official capacity he had offered for the bandit, dead or alive. And subsequently on the 5th of May, 1854, the Legislature of California, considering that his truly valuable services, in ridding the country of so great a terror, were not sufficiently rewarded, passed an act granting him an additional sum of five thousand dollars.

Thus briefly and truthfully, have been sketched the crimes and exploits of the most daring robber that ever existed. During his short and bloody career, he displayed qualities of mind and heart, which marked him as an extraordinary man; and the truly wonderful success which attended him in all his undertakings, is without a parallel in the criminal calendar of the world.

Although the death of Joaquin was a severe blow to the robbers, and eventually caused their disbandment, they still continued their depredations in small parties and without any leaders; and for some time carried on their robberies and murders with such untiring determination of purpose, as to cause serious doubts of the decapitation of the *real* Joaquin.

A young man by the name of Mark T. Howe, aged about twenty-two years, left his cabin on the 10th of August to find a horse, and visit a neighboring camp. His partners, thinking he had gone, no suspicion was excited until the 14th, when the person he was going to visit came to see him. His friends then became alarmed and instituted a search, when his body was found about three-quarters of a mile from his cabin, just back of Albany Flat, between Angel's Camp and Carson's Creek. He had been shot in the head and then lassoed; and the body had been dragged by the neck about fifty feet and secreted in the chaparral bushes, after being robbed of three or four hundred dollars.

Another man was found murdered soon after, below Robinson's Ferry on the Stanislaus river. Some of the bandits had been seen around there just previous, and had gone north to San Antonio. These bandits were Sevalio and five others, who were committing depredations along by San Antonio, El Dorado and the Mountain Ranch.

At San Andreas, on the 15th of August, a Mexican, who had for a long time lent constant aid to the Americans in detecting horse thieves, received caution that the band of Murieta intended to have his life for betraying them to the Americans, and distinctly described one of the gang who was deputed to assassinate him, and advised him to be on his guard. Accordingly on the day mentioned as the intended victim was quietly amusing himself with a game of cards, the assassin and robber entered the room, and was observed to have his hand upon his pistol. Thus was instantly perceived by the Mexican, who dropped his cards saying, "I cannot play any more," and went into another room. Procuring a long knife, he went directly up to the bandit, challenged him with his intention, and before he could use his pistol, plunged his knife through and through him. The Mexican then delivered himself up to Judge Taliaferro, who, on hearing satisfactory evidence to substantiate the above, discharged him.

Some time in 1854, the head of the bandit was sold by Deputy Sheriff Harrison, under an attachment for debts contracted by the person in whose charge it had been placed for exhibition.

It was offered at public sale, and while the bids were being made, an Irishman with considerable indignation exclaimed:

"Oh! bad luck to you for selling your fellow man's head. Sure and you'll never have any good luck as long as you live!"

The bids at this point had run up to $63, and the

salesman, struck somewhat aback by the remark just made, suddenly brought down the hammer at that price.

Harrison subsequently committed suicide; and the purchaser, a gunsmith known as "Natchez" was accidentally killed some time afterwards, by leaving a loaded pistol in a show case.

In writing the history of this notorious robber, facts have been given, and though perhaps colored, they are nevertheless facts, which thousands who are now residents of the State, are cognizant of, and in reading, have no doubt had many events brought vividly to their minds which transpired in the localities where they were in the years '51, '52, and '53. But little doubt exists in the writer's mind that many persons who are mentioned in the advertisements headed "Information Wanted," and emanating, perhaps, from a mother enquiring for her son, or a wife for her husband, have been the victims of the bandit Joaquin.

John R. Ridge, *The Life and Adventures of Joaquin Murieta the Celebrated California Bandit*. Revised and enlarged by the author, the late John R. Ridge. In *The Lives of Joaquin Murieta and Tiburcio Vasquez: The California Highwaymen*. Third edition. San Francisco: F. MacCrellish & Co. 1874 [1871]. Pgs. 3, 5–6, 7–8, 17–19, 33–34.

Ridge's preface to the posthumously published "third" (actually the second) edition of his novel claims that his own "revised and enlarged" edition is motivated by a desire to correct the "crude interpolations" of plagiarized editions such as the California Police Gazette's.

"Author's Preface to the Present Edition": The continued and steady demand for the "Life and Adventures of Joaquin Murieta" induces the author to issue a third edition, revised and enlarged, according to the scope of additional facts, the knowledge of which has been acquired since the publication of preceding editions. This would seem to be the more necessary, as a matter of justice both to the author and the public, inasmuch as a spurious edition has been foisted upon unsuspecting publishers and by them circulated, to the infringement of the author's copyright and the damage of his literary credit—the spurious work, with its crude interpolations, fictitious additions and imperfectly disguised distortions of the author's phraseology, being by many persons confounded with the original performance.

Ridge's enlarged edition includes additional details about Murieta's courtship of Rosita in Sonora.

The first considerable interruption in the general smooth current of his existence, occurred in the latter portion of his seventeenth year. Near the rancho of his father resided a "packer," one Feliz, who, as ugly as sin itself, had a daughter named Rosita. Her mother was dead, and she, although but sixteen, was burdened with the responsibility of a housekeeper in their simple home, for her father and a younger brother, whose name will hereafter occasionally occur in the progress of this narration. Rosita, though in humble circumstances, was of Castilian descent, and showed her superior origin in the native royalty of her look and general dignity of her bearing. She was of that voluptuous order to which so many of the dark-eyed daughters of Spain belong, and the rich blood of her race mounted to cheeks, lips and eyes. Her father doted upon and was proud of her, and it was his greatest happiness, on returning from occasional packing expeditions through the mountains of Sonora (he was simply employed by a more wealthy individual) to receive the gentle ministries of his gay and smiling daughter. Joaquin having nothing to do but ride his father's horses, and give a general superintendence to the herding of stock upon the rancho, was frequently a transient caller at the cabin of Feliz, more particularly when the old man was absent, making excuses for a drink of water or some such matter, and prolonging his stay for the purpose of an agreeable chit-chat with the by no means backward damsel. She had read of bright and handsome lovers, in the stray romances of the day, and well interpreted, no doubt, the mutual emotions of loving hearts. Indeed Nature herself is a sufficient instructor, without the aid of books, where tropic fire is in the veins, and glowing health runs hand in hand with the imagination. It was no wonder, then, that the youthful Joaquin and the precocious and blooming Rosita, in the absence, on each side, of all other like objects of attraction, should begin to feel the presence of each other as a necessity. They loved warmly and passionately. The packer being absent more than half the time, there was every opportunity for the youthful pair to meet, and their intercourse was, with the exception of the occasional intrusion of her brother Reyes, a mere boy, absolutely without restraint. Rosita was one of those beings who yield all for love, and, ere, she took time to consider of her duties to society, to herself, or to her father, she found herself in the situation of a mere mistress to Joaquin. Old Feliz broke in at last, upon their felicity, by a chance discovery. Coming home one day from a protracted tour in the mountains, he found no one in the cabin but his son Reyes, who told him that Rosita and Joaquin had gone out together on the path leading up the little stream that ran past the dwelling. Following up the path indicated, the old man came upon the pair, in a position, as Byron has it in the most diabolical of his works, "loving, natural and Greek." His rage knew no bounds, but Joaquin did not tarry for its effects. On the contrary, he fled precipitately from the scene. Whether he showed a proper regard for the fair Rosita in so doing, it is not our province to discuss. All we have to do is state what occurred, and leave moral discrepancies to be harmonized as they best may. At any rate, the loving girl never blamed him for his conduct, for she took the earliest opportunity of a moonlight night, to seek him at his father's rancho, and throw herself into his arms.

About this time, Joaquin had received a letter from a half brother of his, who had been a short time in California, advising him by all means to hasten to that region of romantic adventure and golden reward. He was not long in preparing for the trip. Mounted upon a valuable horse, with his mistress by his side upon another, and with a couple of packed mules before him, laden with provisions and necessaries, he started for the fields of gold. His journey was attended with no serious difficulties, and the trip was made with expedition.

Ridge's revisions produced a more graphic account of the assault on Murieta and Rosita—one in which Rosita fights back against their attackers.

[. . .] As might have been expected, the young Mexican indignantly remonstrated against such an outrage. He had learned to believe that to be an American was to be the soul of honor and magnanimity, and he could hardly realize that such a piece of meanness and injustice could be perpetrated by any portion of a race whom he had been led so highly to respect. His remonstrations only produced additional insult and insolence and finally a huge fellow stepped forward and struck him violently in the face. Joaquin, with an ejaculation of rage, sprang toward his bowie-knife, which lay on the bed near by where he had carelessly thrown it on his arrival from work, when his affrighted mistress, fearing that his rashness, in the presence of such an over-powering force might be fatal to him, frantically seized and held him. At this moment his assailant again advanced, and, rudely throwing the young woman aside, dealt him a succession of blows which soon felled him, bruised and bleeding, to the floor. Rosita, at this cruel outrage, suddenly seemed transformed into a being of a different nature, and herself seizing the knife, she made a vengeful thrust at the American. There was fury in her eye and vengeance in her spring, but what could a tender female accomplish, against such ruffians? She was seized by her tender wrists, easily disarmed, and thrown fainting and helpless upon the bed. Meantime Joaquin had been bound hand and foot by others of the party, and, lying in that condition he saw the cherished companion of his bosom deliberately violated by these very superior specimens of the much vaunted Anglo-Saxon race!

In this interpolated passage, Ridge depicts a frontierswoman whose skills at riding, roping, and shooting—in addition to her independent and vengeful character— approximate those of Joaquin and his men.

Residing in the vicinity of Hamilton was a hunter, who was known by the simple name of "Peter." He was half Wyandot and half French, and had two daughters, aged respectively eighteen and sixteen. Old Peter was probably the most honest man in all that section of country. Ever since the death of his wife—half French and half Wyandot like himself—which had happened in Iowa many years before the time of his introduction to the reader, he had followed the life of a trapper and hunter, taking his two girls along with him. He had remained some years in the Rocky Mountains, and thence had ranged down by gradual removes, into California. He had horses, a heavy tent, plenty of clothing, and a purse he earned solely by hunting, there being a good cash market for all the venison and bear meat which he could furnish. Peter prided himself upon two things, his own honesty and the virtue of his daughters. They were very handsome girls, and, although trained up in the wilderness, yet they had sufficiently trod the confines of civilization to know something of the refining effects. Besides, their father was by no means a savage, having received the rudiments of a French education in his youth, and having mingled with the better class of the border citizens of the United States to an extent which enabled him to speak pretty good English, and to act very much like a white man. But the Indian instinct was strong, both in himself and his daughters, the elder of whom was a dead shot with the rifle and a splendid rider, after the fashion of Indian women, to wit astraddle. She had learned also to thrown the lasso, and had more than once brought into camp wild elks, lassoed around the horns and towed at her saddle bow. Strange as this may seem, it is literally true, and there are many persons now living in California who remember the girl and her feats[. . . .]

A couple of the bandits were one morning galloping over the plain, in the direction of a band of loose horses, with a view of lassoing one or two of them, when a huge elk rapidly crossed the line of their progress. The animal was making the best speed he could, and well he might, for not more than fifty yards behind there came thundering after him a mounted figure, with disheveled hair and eager eyes and urgent pressings of the pursuing steed. It was the old hunter's daughter, lasso in hand enjoying her favorite pastime of elk-chasing. It may well be conjectured that the bandits were somewhat astonished at this unusual sight, for they had never seen or heard of this extraordinary maiden before. Neither the elk nor the girl paid any attention to them, but dashed on, pursued and pursuing. The robbers, exhilarated by the spectacle, put spurs to their horses and followed in the chase. Onward sped the wild hunter for a mile or more, till now she gains upon the panting beast, reaches within twenty or thirty feet of him, whirls the adjusted loop around and around her head to give it impetus and lets loose the springing coil. Forth it flies on its lengthened mission, and the noose drops down over the branching horns. The well-trained mustang stops short in his tracks, the cord tightens at the saddle-bow, and the flying elk, suddenly jerked backward, falls heavily to the ground. With a shout of applause the robbers recognize the capture and rein their chargers to the spot. Addressing the girl in Spanish, they found she spoke English, and so conversed with her moderately well in that language. The elk being somewhat refractory, they politely offered to help her home with it, and did so, driving it forward while she galloped on ahead. Arriving at her father's camp, it was courtesy to ask the strangers to alight and refresh themselves. They partook of the wholesome repast spread before them by the younger sister, and had finished their last cup of coffee, when old Peter entered. He looked at his new-found guests with a degree of suspicion, and saluted them but coldly. He took no apparent interest in the rehearsal of his daughter's adventure, and, when the strangers arose to depart he did not ask them to call again. One of them, however, the smooth spoken and graceful Claudio, did call the next day, and old Peter peremptorily ordered him away. There was something in the old man's look that even as brave a scoundrel as Claudio did not like unnecessarily to parley with, and thinking "discretion the better part of valor," he left. Old Peter, it seems, knew instinctively that he was a rascal, and was not disposed to waste any ceremonious courtesy upon him.

After the expiration of a few days, the young Diana concluded to ride over into the woods that skirt Butter Creek, a clear, pebbly-bottomed stream that empties into the Feather River, some distance above Hamilton. She took her rifle with her—a small-bored silver-mounted piece, with an elegant curly maple stock—thinking that she would bring in a number of gray squirrels with which the grounds abounded, for the purpose of converting them into a pot-pie. The sharp crack of her rifle was the death-knell of many an "adjidaumo," and soon, with a string of the bushy-tailed "varmints," at her saddle-bow, she grew weary of the sport, and reclined for a brief rest upon a plot of dry grass underneath an oak tree, leaving her docile pony to feed at his discretion in the neighborhood. It was not long before she fell asleep. How long she had slumbered she could not say, but she was suddenly awakened by a strong pressure upon her wrists, and opening her eyes in a fuller consciousness, she found herself in the grasp of a powerful man. It was the late companion of Claudio, in the matter of the elk adventure and the subsequent repast at old Peter's camp. The villain had secured the girl's wrists with a piece of cord, and now held a knife at her throat, threatening to kill her instantly if she dared to scream out. Nevertheless she did scream, until a gag was thrust into her mouth by a second party whom she had not until then discovered, and who proved to be Claudio. The two were proceeding to drag the terrified girl into an adjacent thicket, rendered well nigh impervious by a mazy entanglement of wild pea vines, when a horseman dashed up, and cocking his revolver, commanded the rascals to desist. The girl was surprised to see that they instantly obeyed. She was unbound, her rifle restored to her and her pony led to where she was standing. After she was mounted, and on the point of departing, her strange rescuer rode closely up to her and said:

"Young woman, you've heard of Joaquin Murieta. I'm the man. When you hear people abusing me, hereafter, perhaps you'll think I'm not quite so big a scoundrel as they say I am, after all. Now, hurry home, before some other danger overtakes you."

With a grateful heart, the maiden bade him adieu, and galloped off. When at a distance of about a hundred yards, the group still gazing at her, she suddenly halted, and turned around as if to come back, but stood still, facing them. While they were wondering what on earth she could be at, they soon perceived that she was deliberately leveling her rifle to draw a "bead" on some one of the party. Claudio instinctively wheeled from the front of the tree, where he was standing, with a sudden effort to slide behind it, when the rifle cracked, and the bark flew from the exact spot at which he would have been struck to the heart if he had remained a moment longer. With a sharp feminine whoop and a gay laugh of defiance, the spirited damsel put wings to her horse's feet and was soon out of sight.

In the following interpolated passage, Ridge digresses from the novel's plot to represent Native people in California (whom he refers to derogatorily as "Diggers") as laughable, small, and servile inferiors. He also distinguishes the "Indian village" from the ancient sculptures and pottery of an earlier indigenous civilization, gesturing toward the civilizational potential of Native Americans even as he rehashes the myth of the "vanishing" Native.

On the edge of the big cauldron . . . the party saw tracks of naked feet, and the bones of rabbits, "and such small deer," which had been apparently cooked on the heated rocks that form the rim of the cavern. There was, doubtless, a tribe of people somewhere in the vicinity who adopted this unique mode of converting the sublime and terrible into the useful. Following the tracks over the crispy ground, and circling

the bed of an extensive lagoon, now dry, they reached a
footpath and descended suddenly, and with a transition
truly wonderful, into an exceedingly beautiful valley; and
here was an Indian village. The inhabitants were entirely
naked, men, women and children, of pigmy size, very dirty,
and altogether a very inferior specimen of the sufficiently
inferior Root Digger race of California. This tribe live on
lizards, crickets, roots and worms, fish and occasional rabbits which they snare. Giving these poor creatures a few
presents, the bandits passed on in the path which led
through the village, and reaching the pine-clad spurs of the
eastern slope, were gratified with the sight of what is now
known as Owen's Lake, a body of water filling a huge basin
scooped out for it in the elevated land. It is forty miles long
and from five to ten miles wide. The waters are clear and
brackish, and abound in fish. On one of the streams putting
into this lake the robbers fixed their camp. They were supplied with fish by the Indians, and hunters of the party
brought from the hills, not unfrequently, hams of deer and
antelope. Here the robbers rested and luxuriated, converting the Indians into servants, laughing at their oddities, and
riding or strolling around at their pleasure. In one of his excursions out into the weird realm, upon whose confines he
was quartered, Joaquin noticed on a wall of cliffs sculp-
tured figures, of life size, of men and animals. They appeared to be ancient, and rude as they were, were certainly
above any art in the possession of the miserable race then
living in those parts. He also found, in an obscure crevice, a
rough earthern pot, in which a horned frog had taken up
his abode. For how many centuries he had lived there, a
venerable hermit, it would be hard to tell. Similar earthen
pots have since been found in the neighborhood, and ancient burial places are visible, with circular mounds of
stones heaped upon them, about ten feet in diameter, and
mouldy with time.

Cincinnatus H. Miller, "Joaquin," *Joaquin et al.* Portland, OR:
S. J. McCormick, Publisher, 1872. Pgs. 6–10.

*The California poet Cincinnatus Heine Miller
(1837–1913) wrote under the pen name "Joaquin
Miller" because he was frequently identified with his
popular romantic poem, "Joaquin Murietta." Miller's poem frames Murieta as a nostalgic figure from
California's past, contrasting his exploits with a
peaceful description of ships traversing San Francisco Bay. This excerpt from the poem describes its
subject on horseback, defying his pursuers in a manner reminiscent of the famous painting by Charles
Nahl.*

*What rider rushes on the sight
Adown yon rocky long defile
Swift as an eagle in his flight—
Fierce as a winter's storm at night—
In terror born on Sierra's height,
Careening down some yawning gorge?
His face is flushed, his eye is wild,
And 'neath his courser's sounding feet—
A glance could barely be more fleet—
The rocks are flashing like a forge.
Such reckless rider! I do ween
No mortal man his like has seen.
And yet, but for his long serape
All flowing loose and black as crape,
And long silk locks of blackest hair
All streaming wildly in the breeze,
You might believe him in a chair,
Or chatting at some country Fair
With friend or senorita fair,
He rides so grandly at his ease.*

But now he grasps a tighter rein—
A red rein wrought in golden chain—
And in his heavy stirrup stands—
Half turns and shakes a bloody hand
And hurls imaginary blows
And shouts defiance at his foes—
Now lifts his broad hat from his brow
As if to challenge fate, and now
His hand drops to his saddle-bow
And clutches something gleaming there
As if to something more than dare—
While checks the foe as quick as though
His own hand rested on each rein.
The stray winds lift the raven curls—
Soft as a fair Castilian girl's—
And press a brow so full and high,
Its every feature does belie
The thought, he is compelled to fly.
A brow as open as the sky,
On which you gaze and gaze again
As on a picture you have seen
That seems to hold a tale of woe—
Or wonder—you would seek to know.
A brown cut deep, as with a knife,
With many a dubious deed in life;
A brow of blended pride and pain,
And yearnings for what should have been.

He grasps his gilded gory rein,
And wheeling like a hurricane,
Defying flood, or stone, or wood,
Is dashing down the gorge again.
O never yet has prouder steed
Borne master nobler in his need.

There is a glory in his eye
That seems to dare, and to defy
Pursuit, or time, or space, or race.
His body is the type of speed,
While from his nostril to his heel
Are muscles as if made of steel.
He is not black, nor gray, nor white,
But 'neath that broad serape of night,
And locks of darkness streaming o'er,
His sleek sides seem a fiery red,
Though maybe red with gore.
What crimes have made that red hand red?
What wrongs have written that young face
With lines of thought so out of place?
Where flies he? And from where has fled?
And what his lineage and race?
What glitters in his heavy belt
And from his furred catenas gleam?
What on his bosom that doth seem
A diamond bright or dagger's hilt?
The iron hoofs that still resound
Like thunder from the yielding ground
Alone reply; and now the plain,
Quick as you breathe and gaze again,
Is won. Pursuit is baffled and in vain.

From Johnston McCulley, *The Mark of Zorro* (1919)

This excerpt from the first novel featuring Zorro echoes Murieta's acts of revenge against both government authorities and men who betray his trust. Zorro also shares Murieta's bravado when confronting and escaping his enemies.

CHAPTER 23
More Punishment

Señor zorro rode quickly to the crest of the hill beneath which was the pueblo, and there he stopped his horse and looked down at the village.

It was almost dark, but he could see quite well enough for his purpose. Candles had been lighted in the tavern, and from the building came the sounds of raucous song and loud jest. Candles were burning at the presidio, and from some of the houses came the odor of cooking food.

Señor Zorro rode on down the hill. When he reached the edge of the plaza he put spurs to his horse and dashed up to the tavern door, before which half a dozen men were congregated, the most of them under the influence of wine.

"Landlord!" he cried.

None of the men about the door gave him particular attention at first, thinking he was but some *caballero* on a journey wishing refreshment. The landlord hurried out, rubbing his fat hands together, and stepped close to the horse. And then he saw that the rider was masked, and that the muzzle of a pistol was threatening him.

"Is the *magistrado* within?" Señor Zorro asked.

"*Si, señor!*"

"Stand where you are and pass the word for him. Say there is a *caballero* here who wishes speech with him regarding a certain matter."

The terrified landlord shrieked for the *magistrado*, and the word was passed inside. Presently the judge came staggering out, crying in a loud voice to know who had summoned him from his pleasant entertainment.

He staggered up to the horse, and put one hand against it, and looked up to find two glittering eyes regarding him through a mask. He opened his mouth to shriek, but Señor Zorro warned him in time.

"Not a sound, or you die," he said. "I have come to punish you. Today you passed judgment on a godly man who was innocent. Moreover, you knew of his innocence, and his trial was but a farce. By your order he received a certain number of lashes. You shall have the same payment."

"You dare—"

"Silence!" the highwayman commanded. "You about the door there—come to my side!" he called.

They crowded forward, the most of them *peons* who thought that here was a *caballero* who wished something done and had gold to pay for it. In the dusk they did not see the mask and pistol until they stood beside the horse, and it was too late to retreat then.

"We are going to punish this unjust *magistrado*," Señor Zorro told them. "The five of you will seize him now and conduct him to the post in the middle of the plaza, and there you will tie him. The first man to falter receives a slug of lead from my pistol, and my blade will deal with the others. And I wish speed, also."

The frightened *magistrado* began to screech now.

"Laugh loudly, that his cries may not be heard," the highwayman ordered; and the men laughed as loudly as they could, albeit there was a peculiar quality to their laughter.

They seized the *magistrado* by the arms and conducted him to the post and bound him there with thongs.

"You will line up," Señor Zorro told them. "You will take this whip, and each of you will lash this man five times. I shall be watching, and if I see the whip fall lightly once I shall deal out punishment. Begin."

He tossed the whip to the first man, and the punishment began. Señor Zorro had no fault to find with the manner in which it was given, for there was great fear in the hearts of the *peons*, and they whipped with strength, and willingly.

"You, also, landlord," Señor Zorro said.

"He will put me in *cárcel* for it afterward," the landlord wailed.

"Do you prefer *cárcel* or a coffin, *señor*?" the highwayman asked.

It became evident that the landlord preferred the *cárcel*. He picked up the whip, and he surpassed the *peons* in the strength of his blows.

The *magistrado* was hanging heavily from the thongs now. Unconsciousness had come to him with about the fifteenth blow, more through fear than through pain and punishment.

"Unfasten the man," the highwayman ordered.

Two men sprang forward to do his bidding.

"Carry him to his house," Señor Zorro went on.

"And tell the people of the *pueblo* that this is the manner in which Señor Zorro punishes those who oppress the poor and helpless, who give unjust verdicts, and who steal in the name of the law. Go your ways."

The *magistrado* was carried away, groaning, consciousness returning to him now. Señor Zorro turned once more to the landlord.

"We shall return to the tavern," he said. "You will go inside and fetch me a mug of wine, and stand beside my horse while I drink it. It would be only a waste of breath for me to say what will happen to you if you attempt treachery on the way."

But there was fear of the *magistrado* in the landlord's heart as great as his fear of Señor Zorro. He went back to the tavern, and he hurried inside, as if to get the wine. But he sounded the alarm.

"Señor Zorro is without," he hissed at those nearest the table. "He has just caused the *magistrado* to be whipped cruelly. He has sent me to get him a mug of wine."

Then he went on to the wine cask and began drawing the drink as slowly as possible.

There was sudden activity inside the tavern.

Some half dozen *caballeros* were there, men who followed in the footsteps of the governor. Now they drew their blades and began creeping toward the door, and one of them who possessed a pistol and had it in his sash, drew it out, saw that it was prepared for work, and followed in their wake.

Señor Zorro, sitting his horse some twenty feet from the door of the tavern, suddenly beheld a throng rush out at him, saw the light flash from half a dozen blades, heard the report of a pistol, and heard a ball whistle past his head.

The landlord was standing in the doorway, praying that the highwayman would be captured, for then he would be given some credit, and perhaps the *magistrado* would not punish him for having used the lash.

Señor Zorro caused his horse to rear high in the air, and then raked the beast with the spurs. The animal sprang forward, into the midst of the *caballeros*, scattering them.

That was what Señor Zorro wanted. His blade already was out of its scabbard, and it passed through a man's swordarm, swung over and drew blood on another.

He fenced like a maniac, maneuvering his horse to keep his antagonists separated, so that only one could get at him at a time. Now the air was filled with shrieks and cries, and men came tumbling from the houses to ascertain the cause of the commotion. Señor Zorro knew that some of them would have pistols, and while he feared no blade, he realized that a man could stand some distance away and cut him down with a pistol-ball.

So he caused his horse to plunge forward again, and before the fat landlord realized it, Señor Zorro was beside him, and had reached down and grasped him by the arm. The horse darted away, the fat landlord dragging, shrieking for rescue and begging for mercy in the same breath. Señor Zorro rode with him to the whipping-post.

"Hand me that whip!" he commanded.

The shrieking landlord obeyed, and called upon the saints to protect him. And then Señor Zorro turned him loose, and curled the whip around his fat middle, and as the landlord tried to run he cut at him again and again. He left him once to charge down upon those who had blades and so scatter them, and then he was back with the landlord again, applying the whip.

"You tried treachery!" he cried. "Dog of a thief! You would send men about my ears, eh? I'll strip your tough hide—"

"Mercy!" the landlord shrieked, and fell to the ground.

Señor Zorro cut at him again, bringing forth a yell more than blood. He wheeled his horse and darted at the nearest of his foes. Another pistol-ball whistled past his head, another man sprang at him with blade ready. Señor Zorro ran the man neatly through the shoulder and put spurs to his horse again. He galloped as far as the whipping-post, and there he stopped his horse and faced them for an instant.

"There are not enough of you to make a fight interesting, *señores*," he cried.

He swept off his sombrero and bowed to them in nice mockery, and then he wheeled his horse again and dashed away.

Notes

1. *Rinaldo Rinaldini:* The chivalrous hero of *The Robber Captain* (1797), a novel by the German author Christian August Vulpius.
2. *war with Mexico:* The US-Mexico War (1846–48). See Introduction, page xvii.
3. *Castilians:* An ethnic group in Castile, in central Spain.
4. *Mexiques:* Mexicans.
5. *"monte":* A card game. Either the con game three-card monte (in which the dealer moves three cards around and the mark attempts to keep track of one of the cards), or a game of chance in which the dealer takes four cards, returns them to the deck, and flips cards until finding one that matches one of the original four.
6. *Padre Jurata:* Celedonio Dómeco de Jarauta (1814–48) was a Catholic priest who organized guerrilla companies during the US-Mexico War. After the war, he opposed the Treaty of Guadalupe-Hidalgo and revolted against the Mexican government. He was captured and executed as a revolutionary.
7. *rancheros:* Wealthy property owners who held land grants (*ranchos*) in perpetuity in Alta California under Spanish and Mexican rule. After the United States acquired California in 1848, US settlers contested many of the rancheros' claims.
8. *fandango:* A couples dance originating in Spain.
9. *"the peaceful / Homes of men":* In 1847, *Hunt's Merchant's Magazine* published an article about Pittsburgh, whose inhabitants "by their own efforts and industry have raised up

a great city on these Western waters, and converted a wilderness into the peaceful homes of men . . ."

10. *Arroyo Cantoova:* Arroyo de Cantua [Cantua Creek] in present-day Fresno County. A historical marker at the site identifies it as the "HEADQUARTERS OF NOTORIOUS BANDIT JOAQUIN MURIETA."

11. *express rider:* Mail carrier.

12. *Tejon Indians:* The Tejon nation, but possibly also a reference to the inhabitants of the Sebastian Indian Reservation (commonly known as the Tejon Indian Reseervation) established by the 1851 Tejon Treaty.

13. *Sapatarra:* Possibly a reference to Antonio Zapatero, a mission-educated Indian of mixed Kitanemuk and Hometwoli Tokuts ancestry. The Tejon Treaty was signed in a house built by Zapatero.

14. *tête-a-tête:* A one-on-one interaction (French).

15. *bump of caution:* A reference to phrenology, a nineteenth-century pseudo-science that attributed personal characteristics to features of a person's head.

16. *"greasers":* A racial slur for Mexicans popularized during the US-Mexican War, possible derived from the work of greasing wagons and animal hides.

17. *arroyo:* A brook or a dry stream bed that seasonally fills up (Spanish).

18. *Celestials:* A nineteenth-century term for Chinese people, derived from the translation of China as "Celestial Empire."

19. *no respecter of persons:* A reference to the idea that divine judgment is impartial. See the *King James Bible, Acts* 10:34 and *Romans* 2.11.

20. *long tail:* During the Manchu dynasty in China, men were required to wear their hair in a braided queue as a sign of loyalty.

21. *Grandee:* A high-ranking Spanish aristocrat.

22. *General Vallejo's:* Mariano Guadalupe Vallejo (1807–90) was a *Californio* military officer and state senator.

23. *tules:* A species of sedge native to many freshwater marshes in North America.

24. *Byron:* George Gordon Byron (1788–1824), known as Lord Byron, was an English Romantic poet.

25. *"Woman's tears . . . unman in death":* From Lord Byron, "Euthanasia" (1912).

26. *golden tree of the Hesperides:* In Greek mythology, the

garden of the Hesperides is the site of a tree with golden apples that impart immortality. The Hesperides are nymphs of the evening or sunset.

27. *Bucephalus:* The horse of the Macedonian emperor Alexander the Great.

28. *"let loose for a thousand years":* In the New Testament book of *Revelation*, Satan is said to be bound for 1,000 years prior to being set loose upon the nations.

29. *digger-trail:* A trail used by people indigenous to the land that became the state of California. Among California's settlers, "digger" was a racial slur for Indigenous people who acquired sustenance by hunting and gathering.

30. *stereotyped jokes:* A "stereotype" is a type of printing plate widely that was widely used in the nineteenth-century for mechanical reproduction.

31. *Senati:* A notorious bandit active in California during the 1850s.

32. *yager:* A jaeger (German) is a short-barreled rifle.

33. *Alcalde:* A government official in a Spanish town, or a Native official at a Spanish mission.

34. *California trial:* Extrajudicial "trials" without due process were common in the early years of California under US rule.

35. *Cherokee Flat:* An area in Butte County, California, formerly inhabited by the Maidu nation and settled by a group of Cherokee prospectors in 1849.

36. *Foreign Miners' Licenses:* A reference to California's Foreign Miners Tax, a $20 monthly tax on foreign miners first enacted in 1850, repealed in 1851, and reenacted in 1852. The law was modified to exempt any "free white person," and the tax was collected primarily from Mexican, South American, and Chinese miners.

37. *"Digger-Express":* A phrase (incorporating the derogatory term "digger") for mail carried by a person indigenous to the land that became the state of California.

38. *Judge Lynch:* A personification of lynch law, or extrajudicial trials and executions.

39. *Belshazzar's:* In the Old Testament book of *Daniel*, Belshazzar was a co-regent of Babylon whose knees shook with fear when he saw a hand writing on a wall that prophesized the fall of Babylon.

40. *Cherokee superstition . . . silver bullet:* This was a widespread and longstanding belief seen in European stories

about supernatural creatures, such as the Brothers Grimm fairy tale "The Two Brothers" and the eighteenth century legend of the Beast of Gévaudan in France.

41. *cloven-foot:* In Western mythology and iconography, the Devil is frequently associated with cloven feet.

42. *A petition . . . Legislature:* See Introduction, page xx.

43. *Tivola Gardens:* Possibly a reference to the Tivoli gardens of Paris, the last of which was closed in 1842. By the 1850s, "Tivoli gardens" imitating the famous pleasure gardens of that name in Copenhagen, Denmark, and Tivoli, Italy, had been established throughout the United States.

44. *Major Domo:* The head domestic servant for a household.